DEATH IN COLABA BAY

Ambika Subramanian is a storyteller at heart. A Mumbai-born, Sydney-based author, Ambika holds a master's degree from the London School of Economics (LSE), UK.

A keen observer and travel enthusiast, she dons several hats: marketer, community teacher, travel blogger and photographer.

A voracious reader and writer of fiction since her childhood, the love for her hometown, coupled with a passion for mystery, history and adventure led to her debut novel *Death in Colaba Bay: A Colonial Bombay Mystery*.

Praise for the book

It's a tightly plotted novel, with a noir approach. The descriptions of food and the attire of the characters lend authenticity to the setting, while also supporting the unfolding plot. The author's expertise lies in the way she brings alive a bygone era. The everyday details immediately transport the reader to the era of 1898 Bombay.

Ambika describes in detail the elaborate dinners, dazzling outfits, fancy tea parties and well-mannered society, alongside desperate poverty, racism and entrenched misogyny. There is a great sense of place to this book.

As a cinematographer, I could imagine myself transported to Bombay, easily imagining the sights and sounds of the bustling city. The mystery itself is very cleverly done and it brought a more serious edge to the racy read. The pace of the story is just right.

The vibrant characters of Tara and Arun, and the period charm of nineteenth-century Bombay stick in the memory long after the story is told.

—**Ravi K. Chandran**, cinematographer,
Indian Society of Cinematographers (ISC)

The book does an amazing job of recreating an era—complete with the language, places and spaces, social roles and hierarchies and even fashion choices!

I found the plot very engaging. The connections that emerged between various subplots and characters were delightfully surprising. The two central characters, Tara and Arun, are very likeable, and I would like to see their chemistry being explored further. There is definitely something there! I found Tara easier to empathize with and relate to; she is an interesting, intelligent, enterprising and educated woman from that era. There is just something very classy about her personality. With respect to Arun, I am curious to know more—his backstory and motivations.

I like that Ambika chose a women's educational institution as the backdrop for the crime. That allows us to explore the various societal attitudes for/against women's education and advancement. The portrayal of intelligent women (the princesses, Tara and even the victimized girls) and the motivations behind the antagonist's operations brings forth the nuances of this complex issue.

This book is a pleasurable read and reminded me of the Agatha Christie novels that I have always loved.

—**Supriya Rakesh**, author

DEATH IN COLABA BAY

A COLONIAL BOMBAY MYSTERY

AMBIKA SUBRAMANIAN

RUPA

Published by
Rupa Publications India Pvt. Ltd 2021
7/16, Ansari Road, Daryaganj
New Delhi 110002

Sales centres:
Allahabad Bengaluru Chennai
Hyderabad Jaipur Kathmandu
Kolkata Mumbai

Copyright © Ambika Subramanian 2021

All rights reserved.
No part of this publication may be reproduced, transmitted, or stored in a retrieval system, in any form or by any means, electronic, mechanical, photocopying, recording or otherwise, without the prior permission of the publisher.

This is a work of fiction. Names, characters, places and incidents are either the product of the author's imagination or are used fictitiously and any resemblance to any actual person, living or dead, events or locales is entirely coincidental.

ISBN: 978-93-90260-14-0

First impression 2021

10 9 8 7 6 5 4 3 2 1

The moral right of the author has been asserted.

This book is sold subject to the condition that it shall not, by way of trade or otherwise, be lent, resold, hired out, or otherwise circulated, without the publisher's prior consent, in any form of binding or cover other than that in which it is published.

Prologue

Running through the empty streets of Bombay was not something she had ever seen herself doing, even in her wildest dreams. *Oh, why did I not listen to my conscience?* If only she could reach her destination, she would certainly find help.

The steady rhythm of her feet echoed along the cobbled courtyard of St Francis Xavier's Church. Running through the churchyard had seemed a very good idea when she realized she was being followed. She could hear her assailant. Sweat ran down her scared face as she ran towards the main road bisecting the block. She could see the gaslights at a distance. Her heart was running its own marathon and she certainly didn't want a fate similar to the others.

She had been avoiding the truth for a while now and if she didn't reveal everything she knew, she would never be able to stop the ruthless predator. She was ready to face her scarred past and create a safer future for herself and others. Today, she had the opportunity to change the way things played out.

The attacker was gaining on her and she heard his laboured breathing. She saw lights ahead. She burst onto the main road to find a tram hurtling towards her as it turned around the corner. She heard the tram driver yell and horses neigh loudly as the tram braked. She had no time to stop; if she did, the attacker would reach her. Her only option was to cross the street before *he* did. She put in all her effort and ran forward; missing the first set of horses by a few inches. There was a lot of yelling and commotion, but she did not pause to look. Her destination was just a block away and she had to reach it before Death paid a visit.

one

12 June 1898

'You are dead to me, you ungrateful creature.'

Arun woke up gasping for air. The muggy room did not help matters. He pulled himself out of his bed and pushed open the small window overlooking the eastern seafront. He could see the darkened lanes, the now-quiet markets and the gas-lit docks at a distance. A slight breeze carrying the smell of the sea, eminent rain and docks hit him in the face and he gulped in a few lungfuls to ease the ache that was beginning to form behind his eyes. He rubbed the scar on his right temple. Old and unpleasant occurrences brought along the nightmare. All he needed was some time to chase away the remnants of the recurring nightmare that surfaced when he let his guard down.

Arun Kumar Sadashiv Rao Agashe, known to his colleagues as Inspector Arun Rao, was one of the few people who had made it through the Imperial Services examinations and was trained by the elite at the police training school. He had made it through all odds, including that of surpassing British peers who had taken the exam to make it to the academy.

His first posting had been in Poona, a city that was soon transforming into a heart of learning on the west coast. When he received the letter from the police commissioner's office in Bombay a few months ago, asking him to join the force, he couldn't believe his luck. The letter stated that he was being transferred to the police headquarters as Detective Inspector to solve cases that baffled the force and could potentially cause panic among the city's residents.

Ever since he moved from Poona to Bombay, he was swamped with work. Poona had been a good learning ground for him, both in terms of police work as well as managing the different ideologies that existed in an Anglo-Indian society. The Great Indian Plague had taken a toll on the city's people, including Arun. He was glad he was able to make the move to Bombay and work at the well-renowned Bombay Commissioners Office.

Working in a bustling city as a police detective was no mean feat, but Arun enjoyed the pressure. His job profile entailed meeting a vast number of people, which he liked. He felt a sense of satisfaction on seeing crimes curbed and criminals punished. Looking back, he had indeed come a long way from the fields of Venugiri.

Thinking back to the events of the last few days, Arun wondered about the case. Tonight, he hoped to conclude it. Looking at his pocket watch, he was surprised to note the time. *I am due to be at the meeting point in twenty minutes.*

A sudden noise jerked him from his wool-gathering. He quietly turned away from the window and crept towards the door. Someone was on the stairs. The third step before the landing always creaked. The candle had died sometime along his nap. He quietly lit it and proceeded towards the door. Leaving the door unlocked, he stood behind it awaiting the unknown visitor. The doorknob turned and Arun suddenly pulled the door open. The intruder tumbled in with a loud thud. Slamming the door shut, he turned towards the figure, who was now on the floor. 'Show yourself, before I give you a reason to be sorry,' Arun uttered ominously. The figure turned towards him and in the pale candlelight, he saw who it was.

'You?!' he shrieked.

7 June

Lying on the bed, Tara lazily watched the sunlight filter through the trees. Reluctantly she got up and stood at the window, looking out at the city she called home. It was time to get ready for another long day. Oh, how she missed sharing these early hours of the day with Jivan!

Two years had gone by since he passed away. Tara tried to remember her husband's charming smile, his dishevelled hair, the jokes that always put a smile on her face. The memories were starting to fade.

A lawyer from Baroda, Jivan had shown promise and potential early on in his line of work. Tara and he had planned for a life together and shared many a dream—of building their own home, of raising their children and of travelling the world. It was his work that had got him to Bombay, where he was promoted to a junior partner at one of the leading law firms. She often wondered what could have been done to prevent a young, healthy man from dying so tragically. Had he lived, they would have been celebrating his twenty-seventh birthday today.

Tara watched as the sun rose higher. The warm rays gently caressed her cheeks rousing her to a new day.

'Tara, are you awake?' Jolted out of her trance, Tara turned to smile at Radha—her aunt, her friend, her advisor and also the mother she never knew.

'Good morning, Radha maasi. How are you today?' Tara queried.

Radha, Sharada Desai's cousin and closest companion, had become a permanent member of the Desai family over the years. A widow herself, Radha had come to help Sharada with a difficult pregnancy. With Sharada dying after giving birth to Tara, the upbringing of all the Desai children became Radha's responsibility.

'I am good.'

'Are your knees feeling better after that long footbath, Maasi?'

'My knees are better and, yes, the footbath *really* helped. I should rather work and keep myself occupied than brood over my ageing bones.'

Radha had promised her dying cousin to always love and care for the children as her own. This girl with dark, curious eyes and flushed skin was always cheerful and full of excitement, and she tugged at her heartstrings. Radha understood that behind this façade, Tara was restless on many levels. Being a widow at twenty-one was not what she had envisaged for this child. If only she could do something for her.

'Don't you have to be somewhere today? Your father and brothers are already at breakfast,' Radha said with an indulgent smile.

'I will meet them downstairs in half an hour. Let me have a quick bath, get dressed and say my prayer before my day starts to resemble the Bombay Cotton Exchange,' Tara said with a wry smile.

As Radha left, Tara hurriedly headed to the bathroom at the end of the corridor, calling out to her maid to get her clothes ready. Dressed in a pale-yellow sari with the latest Anglo-style jacket blouse that suited her petite frame, her long dark hair neatly tied in a bun, with bangles adorning her wrist and gold earrings catching the rays of the morning sun, Tara walked into the dining room to see her father and brothers having their breakfast.

Seth Moolchand, a successful and philanthropic cotton merchant in Bombay, looked up to see his only daughter walk in. Tara noticed a strange mix of pride and sadness in his eyes. She was glad that her father was there to support her, but she did not want him to be sad for her. She needed him to trust her to take care of herself.

Tara appreciated her father's decision to bring her home to Bombay. Had she been left to face the dictates of society, her in-laws, however progressive, would have eventually bowed to the pressure and she would have been committed to a rough life and seen as a misfortune.

Tara's father had gone through the same grief of losing his life partner and hence, they felt closer. Her father's support meant the world to her. However, she had been itching to do something useful with her life lately. She also knew he secretly hoped she would find a life partner to share her life with again.

'Good morning, Baabuji. Hope your consignment arrived at the docks yesterday.'

'Good morning, Tara. Yes, the consignment arrived last night. Your brothers are heading out soon.'

'Mukund bhai, how was your meeting with the mill owners' association?' Tara asked, smiling at both her brothers.

Mukund Moolchand Desai, the heir to the Desai business, was a handsome man, with intelligent eyes behind round-rimmed spectacles.

'They are still indecisive about collective bargaining with the government. Let us hope they see reason soon enough.'

As a domestic help served her a plate of fruit and breakfast and a cup of hot tea, Tara turned to her younger brother. 'And, Mohan bhai, how was the new play? Was the new actress really as good as the press makes her to be?'

'Good morning, Tara. The play was wonderfully hilarious and the new actress is indeed good and very beautiful too.'

'Tara, will you be visiting the temple to offer alms to the needy on the occasion of Jivan Kumar's birth anniversary?' enquired Mukund.

Tara had been contemplating for a while on how she wanted Jivan to be remembered. She had finally arrived at a decision the previous night, before drifting off to sleep. 'I will be going to the temple, as usual, Bhai. However starting this year, I also plan to set up a scholarship for girls of the city.' Tara was sure she wanted to use her inheritance money for a cause that Jivan and she deeply believed in. She always considered herself lucky to have been educated at a time when sending girls to schools and colleges, was considered a frivolous expense. Rather than simply donating the money to the temple, she hoped to make a difference in the lives of many through this scholarship.

Looking across the table, she caught the eye of her older brother, who had a worried look on his face. 'What is it, Mukund bhai? What has you looking so uncomfortable?'

'Tara, does your plan of setting up the scholarship begin at your alma mater, Ratanbai School for Native Girls?'

Ratanbai School for Native Girls was a native school like many others that had started in the presidencies as a way of educating young Indian boys and girls in the Western system of education without having to compromise the prevalent Indian values and systems. The Bombay Native Education Society, which was set up by prominent businessman Nana Shankersheth—a pioneer in this space—had paved way for many more Indian schools to sprout. Tara was lucky to study in these newly set up native schools.

'How well you know me, Bhai. Yes, I plan to go and meet the headmistress and explain my plan to her. I am sure Mrs Maneckjee will be thrilled to see her student give something back to society.'

'Have you not read the newspapers lately? The school has been in news over the past week.' Tara did not like the tone of disapproval in Mukund's voice. She would rather not share any plans, she thought.

'Yesterday's was the third such incident to have marred the school's reputation. The girls' parents are worried and are planning on pulling their wards out, lest they are targeted too. There is talk of some orthodox Hindoo sections of the society protesting to demand the shutting down of educational institutions for girls. I for one am not sure how the other communities are going to react next. I doubt the Muslim community is very happy with the situation either,' said Mohan.

'I think they might be worried about their madrasas being

targeted next. It is a natural reaction when crime comes calling,' added Radha, who was helping serve breakfast.

'I agree with you, Radha maasi. However, the crime here is not that girls need to be educated. It is about their safety. Unless we have all the perspectives to a situation, we shouldn't jump to any conclusions.'

Displeased at being cut off, Mohan said, 'I doubt Mrs Maneckjee would be interested in discussing a scholarship unless the police find the person behind the crimes.'

Tara had been closely following the events and was looking forward to meeting the headmistress to know more about them. The letter from yesterday was still on her desk.

Mrs Maneckjee definitely needed her help. Her brothers' unwillingness to trust her judgement irked her. Her family was therefore better off without the information that Mrs Maneckjee had reached out to her, she decided. 'Nevertheless, I am sure Mrs Maneckjee would like to see a familiar face and besides, I am a good listener. After assessing the situation in the school, I can decide on discussing the scholarship,' she said, sipping her tea.

The table fell quiet and the only sound was that of everyone contemplating Tara's announcement.

Spying her father getting up from his seat, Tara stood up too. 'Baabuji, please say you have no objection if I take the tram. I will take someone along with me to the temple and then to the school,' Tara pleaded excitedly.

Moolchand wasn't happy about letting his daughter roam the city in crowded trams, especially when they had multiple tongas at home. 'You may go, but take Shankar with you. That way I can rest assured he will keep you out of harm's way in those crowded and slow-moving trams. Make sure you are home for lunch,' Moolchand said, taking his leave.

Tara was excited about her plan, but she could see the unease and concern in her brothers' eyes.

two

7 June

Bombay was a different game. So far, he had never attempted to do this. It was now time to up the stakes and start expanding. When he decided to risk this move, he wasn't sure of the logistics or the ease of execution. Surprisingly, Bombay provided many more avenues to execute his plan. Although the risks were high, he was willing to go beyond his comfort zone.

There were a few hurdles, none that could not be surpassed. His crew knew the drill and had done all the groundwork. He even had some extra hands for special assignments. The year 1894 had been good for him. He had managed to almost pull off the biggest coup of his lifetime; however, life had other plans for him.

He wasn't the one to whine. After all, he was a self-made man. 'And when the time comes, I will be ready with a coup of a different kind. Till then, I will bid my time.'

～

Arun walked into the station house and headed to his desk. On some days, he missed the cool breeze and fresh air of Venugiri. The heat had made him extremely irritable and all he wanted was five minutes of peace before beginning a long day.

Taking his coat off, he hung it on the peg behind his desk and opened the window to let the sea breeze in. The small room was instantly flooded with the smell unique to Bombay—a mixture of sea-dampened earth, flowers and cattle. The din from the market across the road could be heard. The Gulmohar tree outside the window danced gaily, and Arun couldn't help but smile, despite his mood.

Picking up the newspaper, he scanned the front page for updates on the missing girls' case and the only story on it, a short piece below the headlines, was a huge disappointment to him. Another short piece by a local reporter who had been covering the case caught Arun's eye. The report did not cover the facts of the abduction as it happened. The reporter had not even bothered to check with the authorities, if there were any updates or breakthroughs in the case. Instead, it assumed various theories, which in turn, propagated fear and confusion among the public. Such awful misrepresentation of facts would only prove to be counterproductive. *Why don't these reporters pay more attention to the facts?* thought Arun.

The case was still half-baked in Arun's mind. Apart from the time and area where the incidents had taken place, each modus operandi was different.

Naina was kidnapped right after school, around one in the afternoon. It was a Friday and the namaz, midday prayers, had just ceased. The perpetrators had taken the cover of the crowd coming out of the mosque near the school, to nab Naina as she walked the short distance home. According to eyewitnesses, Gauri too was snatched around the same time as she waited for her carriage to pull up in front of the school. She was taken in a carriage that resembled hers. Whoever was orchestrating these crimes had sufficient knowledge about these girls and their whereabouts. Vidya's case was still a mystery. She was last seen walking out of the school towards the temple at the end of the street at around quarter to 1.00 and had gone missing from there. *How did they get her?* he wondered.

'Inspector, the deputy superintendent wants to meet you,' said the constable, Chavan, shaking Arun out of his reverie. Chavan was one of the newly assigned constables at the commissioner's office. He was in his forties with a receding hairline. He was glad to be part of the crime detection unit. During the initial introduction, he had told Arun about his work during the plague and how fighting other kinds of crime was better than herding people towards segregation. Arun folded the newspaper and marched towards the deputy's room. On entering, he was surprised to see another gentleman already seated with the deputy.

'Join us, Rao. Let me introduce you to Inspector Shukla. He is from the Central Provinces and a colleague of Inspector Verma, my army friend.'

Arun sized up his counterpart from the Central Provinces. Shukla was about 30, medium built with a neatly trimmed moustache and a sleek centre-parted hairstyle that looked stylish yet conformed to the police standards. He had an air around him that some women may find charming. They shook hands and Deputy Superintendent Thakore signalled Arun to take a seat next to Inspector Shukla.

'We were just discussing the case. He believes he has information that may be useful to you,' Thakore added.

Arun turned attentive. Any information from Retired Col. Indrajit Singh Thakore was not to be ignored. His military background prepared him for the worst and he was one of the few Indian officers to be appointed to the Bombay headquarters to help maintain law and order. An imposing figure with a booming voice, his neatly trimmed beard and well-tailored clothes added to his personality.

'Inspector Shukla, I am sure it's something important that brings you all the way here from the Central Provinces.' Arun was intrigued to know what information Shukla had that could aid him in the case.

'Inspector Arun, I am here on some personal work. As you are aware, the Bombay newspapers make it to Indore a few days late. It was when Thakorjee mentioned about the case, that I remembered something. It seemed very similar to the ones in the Central Provinces a few years back.'

Arun sat up erect on his chair. This was indeed worrying. *Why had such a piece of information not come to light earlier?*

'Many are still unsolved. My senior, Inspector Verma, who was handling the case in Jaiwar, had made notes,' said Shukla.

'Thank you, Shuklajee. All of the girls who have gone missing belong to one of the prominent native schools in the city and their parents are fraught with worry. Was it the same in the other cases too? Did the other families receive any ransom note?' Thakore queried.

'I am not very sure about all the cases,' hedged Shukla. 'However, during my investigation into one of the cases, I had my suspicion that someone from the palace of Jaiwar was involved.'

Arun and Thakore exchanged puzzled looks.

'I tried digging for more information. But before I could find anything concrete, there was this palace fire. A few people lost their lives even. At that time, a thorough search was carried out. But nothing was found. My senior and I could prove nothing, for lack of evidence. I was transferred to Indore shortly after that. I am not saying the royal family was involved in that case of missing girls in Jaiwar, nevertheless, something did seem fishy.'

Thakore and Arun looked equally pensive.

'I hope that the fire and the royal family of Jaiwar have nothing to do with our case. What we know for now is that since no known ransom demands have been made yet, money is not likely the motive,' said Arun.

Shukla nodded gravely. The men stood up and shook hands. 'I am going to be in Bombay for a couple of more days. If you need anything, you can reach me at the guest house on Picket Lane,' said Shukla, before taking his leave.

'What do you think, Arun?' asked Thakore, after seeing Shukla out. 'Are there any similarities, or is it just a coincidence that similar incidents have happened in the Central Provinces a few years back? Do you really think a royal family would have any connection to a crime of such nature?'

'I am not certain if the fire had anything to do with the abduction in the Central Provinces. But to conclude or disregard without all the facts is not the way I work. Sir, would you be able to arrange for the files from the older case for me to examine?'

At this point, Arun felt anything that could provide a clue was worth investigating. With the third girl abducted the day before, the pressure was mounting. The only common link was the school and to solve this case too he had to start where it all began—from the school.

7 June

Tara always visited the Babulnath temple on days when she felt the need to collect her thoughts. Today was no exception. As she trekked up the hill to the temple, she wondered what could have caused the girls from Ratanbai School to be kidnapped. She was aware that educating girls was still frowned upon by many sections of the society. *Could it be some extremists who decided to abduct the girls to spread fear among parents educating their girls? Was it to discourage those who support the idea of an educated woman? If these indeed were the reasons, why wasn't a demand made? Could there be another angle to this story that no one knows about? Was it something personal?*

Hymns and chantings greeted Tara as she neared the temple's main entrance. Overlooking the Arabian Sea, the temple stood proudly guarding the city she called home. After a long battle for rightful land ownership between the Hindoos and the Parsis, the temple had finally been restored to its former glory. Many men, her father among them, had contributed to the cause.

Most servants accompanied their employers to the temple. The temple tank on the outer fringes of the complex was a favourite spot for the servants to share gossip and a few good laughs. After offering her prayers to the deity and distributing food to the needy, Tara sat down under a tree and watched the proceedings around her with an indulgent smile. Shankar, who had accompanied her, sat on one of the steps of the temple tank and caught up on all the gossip with his peers. She had asked Shankar to find out from the other servants what they had heard or thought of the recent happenings.

A laugh at a distance broke her reverie and Tara looked around to see a man and a young girl of about twelve or thirteen walk up the steps of the temple. The girl was traditionally dressed, covering her head with a dupatta. Tara couldn't make out her features. They were accompanied by a maid and a couple of manservants. The man was tall and muscular. With a strong jaw, long nose and a neatly trimmed beard, he looked regal, and somewhat familiar, too. The pair entered the temple and Tara looked away to see Shankar come her way.

'Who is distracting you, Tara bibi?' enquired Shankar.

'No one in particular, Shankar. I thought I saw someone familiar. Did you find anything useful?'

'The girls were all from progressive families, who could afford to send them to school. You already know that, considering they went to school. They were of almost marriageable age. Not much is known in terms of their names. A few servants haven't been seen in the past few days even at the bazaars. There is a rumour doing the rounds that the abducted girls could belong to one of those families who had employed the now missing servants. They may have decided to stay indoors for fear of these reporters accosting them. One of the maids might know more. I am sure we can extract more information if I were to have a small chat with the lady,' replied Shankar with a twinkle in his eyes.

Shankar had known Tara since she was a toddler. He had

come as a fourteen-year-old to maintain the gardens and tend to the horses in the Desai household. Since then, he had grown to be the man Friday of the family.

'Never mind them, Shankar. We have a lot of work to do before heading home.'

On turning, she saw the girl and the man come out of the temple. Tara recognized the man and called out, 'Yuvraj Jaswant.'

They turned around. 'Tara bai, what a pleasant surprise! I had no idea you were in Bombay. I would have made an effort to visit you sooner,' he said, coming forward to chat with Tara.

'I am the one who is surprised to see you here. Are you visiting or have you moved to Bombay from Jaiwar?'

'I live here now,' said the prince.

'When we met in Baroda a few years ago, you had no plans of moving to a big city.'

Tara noticed the subtle change in Jaswant's and his companion's countenance. She smiled at the girl to ease the discomfort. Jaswant shook his head, 'How rude of me! Tara bai, please meet my sister Shivani Raje Kaushal, Princess of Jaiwar.'

Tara and Shivani greeted each other. 'How do you find the city of Bombay, Shivani Raje?' enquired Tara.

'Please call me Shivani. Raje sounds too formal among acquaintances,' said a shy Shivani.

Tara and Jaswant laughed and the trio continued their discussion as they descended towards the line of tongas.

'So what brings you to our city, Yuvraj?'

'As you are aware, our province is well known for masonry. My family has been a patron of the masons and we trade with many to promote the artwork. The trade has increased ever since I started to involve myself in it fully. With Father busy handling the royal duties, I have started to expand the trade to different parts of the Empire. The Europeans are our biggest clients. Moving to Bombay means I am in the midst of both the financial and logistical end of things.'

'That seems like a good decision. Shivani, are you visiting your brother or do you plan to make this city your home too?'

A hesitant Shivani looked at Jaswant before answering, 'I am here to enrol myself in the English Finishing School. I am to be married early next year.'

Tara, although surprised, congratulated the girl and excused herself. The royal siblings bid adieu promising they would meet her soon, as her father had invited them for dinner.

How typical of Baabuji to invite royalty and not inform the household. I can't wait to see Radha maasi's reaction. Tara smiled slyly and beckoned to Shankar.

Shankar followed the trio accompanied by the royal servants. Tara and he hailed a tonga and instructed the driver to take them to their next destination—Ratanbai School for Native Girls.

Everything was in place. Bombay was indeed proving to be an interesting move. The time for the exchange had been fixed. He could feel the excitement run up his spine. The fact that his plan and method were as unknown as his identity, added an extra thrill to this whole game. He was aware that the police were frantically searching for clues and a motive behind the disappearance of the girls. The hide-and-seek was going to be really interesting! He could almost smell the success of his first Bombay run.

three

7 June

Arun had been reading his notes from the current case. They weren't forming a pattern yet. *Personal vendetta or a bigger plot to shake up the society, what could it be? Could it have something to do with the school and its founders?* He was in the midst of comparing his notes with all the parallel theories he planned to explore, when a constable burst in.

'Sir, a body has been found at Back Bay.'

Arun looked up at Constable Santosh Wagh. Wagh was an energetic young chap who had joined the constabulary as a means to feed his family, like scores of other public servants. Arun knew that Wagh had a keen mind. His theories had helped them crack a few other cases. Coming from the lower rungs of the society, he knew the pulse of the labour class in the city. Arun really appreciated Wagh's 'unofficial' network of informers, or khabris.

'It seems to be the body of one of the missing girls. She has been brought ashore. Dr Webb has been informed and will meet us at the scene.'

Dr Andrew Webb, a distinguished English doctor who had come to Bombay in 1890, worked for the police department. Since his joining, he had worked relentlessly with the police and the coroner, especially during the great plague. His previous knowledge of working with the London police authorities to control the spread of cholera in 1866 helped him during the Bombay plague. At a time when it was considered inhuman to desecrate a body, he was one of the first few who insisted on a post-mortem procedure in case of a sudden or suspicious death.

Arun and Wagh reached the scene to find that the body had been washed onshore a fishing village on the western end of Colaba Causeway. It was 11.00 in the morning and the heat had started to set in. It was almost time for the afternoon market. Many curious fishermen joined the doctor and the police at the shore.

'Do we know who the victim is?' asked Dr Webb.

'I believe her to be one of the missing girls. If I am not wrong, her face matches Naina Mehta's description. What is the cause of death, doctor?'

'It is certainly not suicide. The marks on her arms suggest she was tied up until recently and the bump on her head could be because of a fall. Whether she died before hitting the water or her body was thrown over can only be ascertained after a post-mortem. Prima facie, Rao, you have a suspicious death.'

It was arranged for the body to be transported to the police morgue and Dr Webb left to conduct a detailed post-mortem, promising to send his reports at the earliest.

Arun walked up to the edge. With the waves lapping at the rocky outcrop, he looked out into the sea. The tide was in. *The waves must have carried her body ashore. Where had she fallen from? Was she running to escape from someone or was she dumped into the sea by her captor during her bid to escape?* Now he had more questions than answers and a set of bereaved parents to talk to. *How I wish I had stayed back in Venugiri!*

Mrs Maneckjee, the principal of Ratanbai School for Native Girls, had gathered her students in the common hall for an official address. She informed the girls and staff of the latest abduction and promised to take immediate action against the persons responsible. She urged everyone to be aware and to report anything amiss to her or the school authorities.

Tara was happy on entering her alma mater and seeing the familiar rooms that dotted the long hallway. Ratanbai School for Native Girls, a mainstream school for Indian girls from liberal families, was founded thirteen years ago by Mrs Maneckjee. Housed in the elite quarter of Queens Road, it had steadily established itself as a reputable institution.

Mrs Maneckjee's husband was with the diplomatic service. After his retirement, they returned to Bombay. The school initially had only students from the Parsi community but now included all native communities of Bombay. Tara was from the first batch of non-Parsi students to attend this school.

As Tara waited in the corridor for Mrs Maneckjee to finish her talk, she found herself in the company of a young clerk.

'Can I help you with anything, madam?' he asked.

'Oh, it is nothing. I am here to meet Mrs Maneckjee. I just heard about the abduction.'

'Do you know the girls personally, madam?'

'Well, I have known… Are you new here, Mr…' she trailed off.

'Das,' the young man offered. 'I am a clerk here.'

'Well, that is good. You might be able to help me.'

They had just started to get to the most interesting part of the chat when a flustered Mrs Maneckjee rushed out of the hall and, on seeing Tara, stopped short.

'Mrs Sethia, I am so relieved…' she paused, noticing the clerk. 'Is there anything you need, Mr Das? If not, I would appreciate if you return to your work,' she said in an authoritative tone.

Mumbling an apology, the clerk took off.

Tara followed Mrs Maneckjee into her office. 'Mrs Sethia, it is so good of you to come,' she said in a tired voice.

Tara smiled at her teacher and sat down in one of the French époque armchairs which were scattered around the coffee table. The principal's room was the height of European décor from when the school opened in the late '70s. Her travels as a diplomat's wife had influenced her choices in décor. Mrs Maneckjee looked up and gave a trembling smile. The stress of the past few days had started to show on her face.

'Mrs Maneckjee, do you mind if I call in for some tea?'

'No, of course not!'

Tara got up and rang for some tea for the headmistress and herself. Mrs Maneckjee's office was filled with photos of all her students. She had a corner table with other frames that captured special moments of her students' achievements. Tara noticed her own picture from when she had won the editorial contest hosted by *The Times* in 1892. Her report on the spate of strikes that the mill workers of Bombay had embarked upon, which focussed on the lack of leadership among them, the failure of foresight among mill owners and the consequences was adjudged the winner. When the mill owners and labour associations found out that the winner was a girl, her work was dismissed. The old memories brought a smile on Tara's face. Mrs Maneckjee's loud sigh suddenly broke the silence. Placing the photo back on the table, Tara casually asked, 'Since when did you cease calling me Tara, Mrs Maneckjee?'

'Tara, you haven't changed much from the forthright girl I knew. I have always admired your ability to think rationally and solve problems, even as a student here. I sometimes wonder if marrying into an influential family and your subsequent loss had altered you. But now I can see that you haven't changed, and I am glad you didn't.'

Smiling, Tara took her seat and asked, 'Now that we have my character sketch out of the way, how can I help you in this situation?'

Dr Webb entered his office, which was in the large backyard of the police headquarters. His official quarter was a small cottage nearby and a converted stable served as the surgery or autopsy room. The attendants had brought the body and placed it on the slab. Hot and cold washbasins and all surgical instruments were readied.

The doctor proceeded to dissect the corpse and conduct the usual procedures to determine the cause of death. Arriving in Bombay at the wake of the Great Plague, Dr Webb had since stayed back to assist the police in their cases and was soon planning to run for the post of the official coroner for the Bombay Police.

After ascertaining the cause of the girl's death, he called out to his assistant to send a message to Inspector Arun that the body was ready to be released.

Lighting a cigar in the confines of his home, Dr Webb mused about the loss of such a young life.

~

Everything around her smelt of the sea. When Vidya gained consciousness, she found herself seated with her back against a damp, cold stone wall. Scared and hungry, she squinted in the darkness, searching for a ray of light. Steadying her breathing, she tried to recollect the sequence of events that had led to her current predicament.

As usual, she had left school at quarter to 1.00 and had walked up to the temple to wait for Omkar to arrive. Omkar usually met her and Uma at the temple, from where they walked back home together. Uma usually walked a few paces behind offering them a bit of privacy and, at the same time, keeping up the chaperoning. Uma had not come to school that day and Vidya was finally going to be with Omkar without a chaperone. They were already breaking societal rules by meeting before the wedding; this was even more exciting. Walking quickly, she reached her spot.

I have to thank Uma later for this new sari and jacket that she has let me borrow. It was their betrothal anniversary and she would be meeting Omkar again for dinner at her place. It was almost time, but Omkar had not arrived yet.

'Excuse me, miss, are you waiting for Omkar Sawant?' suddenly someone said from behind.

As she turned around to see who it was, she saw a decent chap dressed in the usual dhoti, coat and cap. 'Who are you?' she asked, nodding.

'Omkar works with me and he asked me to pass on a message to you. He is running late and won't be able to meet you here. He asked me to tell you that he will be waiting at the tram stop instead.'

Omkar is never late. That's strange!

Also, Vidya had to get home before her mother got worried. She thought there will be no harm in meeting him at the tram stop. Thanking the man, Vidya started walking towards the tram stop through the outer fringes of Null Bazaar. The midday market was crowded as usual. Vidya browsed through the variety of wares on sale and wondered what it would be like to be wealthy enough to own those.

A man bumped into her and even before she could scream, a cloth was thrown over her head and she was whisked away into one of the alleys that dotted the bazaar. The heat and the hood added to her fear and discomfort. She heard the voice of the stranger asking his mate to get the bullock cart readied before losing consciousness.

Now, as she recollected the train of events, she realized it was highly stupid of her to have missed so many glaringly obvious clues. After all, why would Omkar tell his colleague about their rendezvous when even their parents didn't know about it?

⁓

Tara was ushered into the home of Kalyanjee Mehta, a local trader. The servant showed her to the receiving room and went in search of the mistress of the house. Tara looked around and seated herself at the divan by the balcony door. This house was not very different from the other missing girls' she had visited prior to this. Ganga Mehta, a lady in her late thirties who was dressed in her sari covering her head, came in. She looked like someone who hadn't slept in a long time.

Tara enquired about the family and how they were coping with the situation. Belonging to the same community meant she knew the Mehtas socially.

'I don't know what to do! It has been four days now and the police have not been able to find anything. My husband and I are very worried. Naina is engaged to be married and her fiancé is due to finish his education and return from Lahore to marry in August. We haven't said anything to the boy's family and hope to get her home before anything untoward happens,' sobbed Ganga.

Tara understood the woman's anguish. A daughter missing from home; if the news was to spread, the family would be publicly humiliated and socially shunned forever.

'Can you tell me how Naina was before she went missing? Was there anything that troubled her? Did she mention anything that might have happened at school?'

'I am not sure how I can help,' Ganga looked up, continuing to sob. 'Naina and I have never been very close. I have also been very busy planning the wedding. I think Kajri might know if there was something. She is our maid and accompanied Naina to and from school.'

'May I speak with Kajri?'

Tara's recent conversation with Mrs Maneckjee had filled in some of the gaps in her own understanding of the situation. Tara was troubled to see her former headmistress in distress. Her idea of visiting the parents of the missing girls was to comfort them and gather as much information as possible. She wanted to piece the entire picture and provide some kind of comfort or closure to her teacher as well as to these baffled and grieving parents.

Although the mother seemed reluctant, Tara knew she wanted her daughter back. So Kajri was called for and Tara asked her the same questions on Naina's recent behaviour and state of mind. Kajri seemed frank and outspoken.

'Naina bibi went to school so that she could ride the tram on the days when the tonga wasn't available. She liked to talk to the other students who travelled by tram to other schools. She always wanted to know more about the world outside of Bombay. The boys who answered were always courteous.'

'Don't you dare say lies, you impudent girl. My daughter did not mingle with boys. Her upbringing doesn't excuse such behaviour,' shrieked Ganga.

Tara hid her smile. This was such a typical case of social outrage. The mother had no clue that her daughter was inquisitive and did not shy away from talking to boys, especially if they had the right information for her. Before Tara could continue with her questioning, there was a knock on the door.

Inspector Arun and Constable Wagh were ushered in, and their presence left Mrs Mehta in a fit of sobbing all over again. Arun and Constable Wagh looked extremely uncomfortable in the company of a sobbing, borderline-hysterical woman flanked by a worried maid and another young woman who looked at them with curious eyes.

Arun decided to go for the direct approach and sat down in the nearest chair. He began, 'Mrs Mehta, can you please call Mr Mehta? I would like to speak with both of you.'

'Sethji is at the shop. I will ask Bandhu to get him,' said Kajri, rushing out of the room.

In the uncomfortable silence, sprinkled with sobs, Arun and Tara sized each other up. Sitting erect on the divan across the room, Tara looked very regal. Simply yet elegantly dressed in a sari draped in the traditional way, with minimal jewellery, the young lady looked more suited to be in a royal court than a small sitting room in the by-lanes of Bombay. *Maybe the Mehtas have royal connections back home*, thought Arun.

Tara found Arun to be unlike most police officers. Slightly taller than most men she knew, Arun's hair was dark and wavy, and in an era of moustaches, he was clean shaven. He had neatly brushed his short-cropped hair and sported the latest trend of short side burns. His hazel eyes added to his intelligent demeanour. He was looking dapper in the standard khaki trousers and a white shirt, visible through the near-unbuttoned collar of his jacket.

Most of the officers Tara had met socially or through Jivan's work were old and inclined to ignore her from their so-called intelligent conversations. With the rapid changes in the Bombay Police, newer and younger officers were joining the ranks and the inspector seemed to be one of them. *Maybe he won't shun or disregard my theories simply because of my gender.*

Kalyanjee Mehta, a man in his late forties, rushed in—all flushed and thirsty. His kurta was drenched in sweat and his turban was askew, confirming the fact that he had arrived hurriedly. 'What is it, Inspector? Do you have news of my daughter?'

Arun stood up and offered his chair to Kalyanjee. Crouching next to him, Arun broke the news without further ado. 'We found a body this morning at Colaba cove. By the looks of it, she might be Naina, your daughter.'

Kalyanjee's and Ganga's shocked expression confirmed that they were expecting their daughter to return soon. Tara looked at them with utmost concern and sympathy.

'I am so very sorry for your loss,' spoke Arun softly. 'The doctor has yet to ascertain the exact cause of death. We are investigating it and would welcome any information that you could give us on why someone would target your daughter. But before that, I need one of you to formally identify her.'

The terrible descent of grief in Kalyanjee's eyes was unbearable.

Societal norms made it so difficult for men to express their emotions, mused Tara. A father should be allowed to grieve for the death of his child. Before she could offer her condolences and console the shocked parents, Ganga fainted and the servants and Kalyanjee rushed to attend to her. Tara stood up and quietly made her way to the door, closely followed by Arun and Constable Wagh.

'Kalyanjee, Constable Wagh will stay here and once Mrs Mehta recovers, he will accompany you to the morgue at the police station. You will have to identify the body. There will be legal formalities. There are a lot of questions to be answered. I will meet you there.'

Kalyanjee instructed the servants to take Ganga inside while he and the inspector exchanged a few parting words, with Arun promising to return later to question the household.

Turning around, Arun found Tara standing a few feet away, waiting for him to finish his discussion with Kalyanjee and Wagh.

Walking up to her, Arun asked, 'Miss, are you a friend of the family?'

'No, Sir. I am an acquaintance and had dropped by to meet with Gangaben and enquire about her daughter's recent disappearance. I was curious to know if there was someone whom her daughter had mentioned or if Naina had witnessed anything that could be connected to her disappearance. I felt if there was indeed another person involved, it was worth investigating.'

'If you aren't family and just a mere acquaintance, who are you and why are you so interested in this case? What is your connection to the disappearance and death of Naina Mehta?' Arun enquired authoritatively.

'I am Tara Bai Sethia, daughter of Moolchandjee Desai,' Tara hesitated before replying. She wanted to show that she was earnestly involved and hence added, 'I am married into the Sethia family of Baroda.'

Arun knew that the Desais were famous cotton merchants in the city and that the Sethias of Baroda was a very well-known family with connections to the royalty. No wonder she had that air about her, supposed Arun.

'I wanted to help because I am a former student of Ratanbai School for Native Girls.'

Arun looked keenly at Tara. She was not lying, but the only way to confirm all of this without causing a scene was accompanying her home and ascertaining the facts.

'Let me escort you back home and maybe you could let me know your thoughts on Naina based on your conversation with Mrs Mehta,' said Arun.

'Do you have a tonga or do we call for one?' asked Tara eagerly, her eyes all lit up.

With an indulgent smile, Arun led her downstairs to the police tonga waiting for them on the street.

Shankar spotted Tara coming out of the building in the company of a smart young man. He waved out to her, before quickly crossing the street.

'Sir, this is Shankar, my father's competent assistant and is accompanying me today.'

'Shankar, I am Inspector Arun Rao,' offered Arun.

Arun—the name suits him, Tara thought to herself. He seemed bright and burning with curiosity as his namesake, the sun. 'The inspector has offered to drop us home. I am sure he wants to ensure I am who I claim to be,' said Tara cheekily as she climbed onto the horse carriage, leaving a chuckling Shankar and a stunned Arun behind.

~

He had no choice but to punish that churlish girl. She wanted to run back home. The exchange was planned. The interested party was waiting at the designated spot. How dare she defy him and try to run away?

Rich Bombay girls can be difficult. Sitting in the comforts of their furnished home, with servants and vehicles to do their bidding, they feel they are protected. Laughing, he walked on; their naivety was their biggest downfall. Educated they might be, but not smart enough to save themselves.

He mourned the loss of the girl. She had almost threatened to end his Bombay dreams. Disappointment was not a new feeling. He was well versed with it. No time for wallowing in pity, it was time to tie up all the loose ends. The plan couldn't be compromised. There was a job to be done, a new girl to be found.

four

7 June

Radha rushed to the door when she saw a police tonga approaching the entrance. Tara was running late and she hoped the girl would come in before the men arrived for lunch. She saw Shankar and another man alight from the carriage. The young officer then helped Tara off the carriage.

Opening the front door, Radha stepped on to the veranda and called out, 'You are running late, Tara. Your father and brothers are expected anytime now.'

Tara smiled at her aunt and introduced Arun to her.

'I met Inspector Rao by chance, and I invited him over for lunch. I hope that won't be a problem for the cook. I am sure Baabuji wouldn't mind either,' she motioned Arun to follow her inside. Shaking his head in disbelief over the surprise invite, Arun followed Tara and Radha and settled himself in the sitting room.

The Desai house was well done up in an eclectic mix of Victorian fashion, yet having the warmth of a typical Indian household. The sitting room had tall glass windows overlooking the sea to let the breeze in. A divan with bright fabric provided the right contrast to the grey carved detailing sofa and Anglo-Indian chairs made of teak accessorized with gold cushions. The diverse mix of two cultures gave it a unique feel.

Radha was pleasantly surprised to see a young officer with so much self-confidence. She also knew her niece was up to something. She decided to take the bull by its horns. 'So, officer, tell me, are you religious?'

'I beg your pardon?' said Arun.

'Well, considering my niece was to be at the temple this morning and you have accompanied her, I assumed you were religious and decided to take some help from the Lord with respect to your cases.'

'Unfortunately, I am not very religious,' Arun smiled sheepishly and replied. 'And by the looks of it, your niece here had other engagements apart from—'

'I am right here,' Tara butted in. 'Both of you need not speak of me in third person.'

'To cut a long story short, I met your niece at one of the victims' houses. She claims to be an acquaintance of the family. And I am really curious to know what she has managed to learn at the girl's place she visited today. I am the officer in charge of the missing girls' case.'

'Now, why on earth are you going about meeting parents of abducted girls?' Radha looked at Tara quizzingly.

'I am helping Mrs Maneckjee, Radha maasi.' Tara told her about how her headmistress had sought her help in assuring the parents that the school was doing its level best to assist the police with their investigations. 'We both happened to be at the Mehtas' residence at the same time,' Tara added.

'To answer your earlier questions, Sir,' said Tara, 'I visited Gauri Deshmukh's family too, prior to meeting the Mehtas. She and Naina disappeared almost at the same time. Her parents were very worried too. They haven't received any ransom note yet and it's been over two days now.'

Arun sat forward clasping his fingers over his knees. Radha listened keenly.

'Her maid, on the other hand, mentioned seeing a young fellow, whom Gauri met many a time on her way to school, outside their house on the day of the abduction. Shankar spoke to the driver and he confirmed seeing the same young man a couple of times around the school on days when he went to pick up Gauri. The driver had even voiced his suspicion to Gauri's father, Deshmukhjee.'

Arun wondered how the police constable who had questioned the staff at the Deshmukh house missed the information about the same person being spotted outside the school. He was surprised that an inexperienced young woman could glean so much over casual conversation, which sometimes even experienced policemen miss out. She was surely an astute person who knew how to navigate the society and get people to talk to her. He had to keep an eye on her, lest she upsets the apple cart.

'Thanks, Mrs Sethia,' said Arun. 'The sketch of this said man is being circulated around Bombay city, the mill districts and docks. We had been informed on our first visit about the same person.'

Tara smiled and continued, 'Well, maybe what you missed during your questioning was that he was spotted around the house at the same time when Gauri was considered missing from school. If he indeed was the person responsible, why would he be near the house around the same time, knowing fully well that Gauri is to be abducted from school?'

Arun had considered the same thing and the only conclusion he could draw was that there was an accomplice who must have committed the actual crime. 'There must be an accomplice then,' Arun shared his view. 'While our mystery man got himself an alibi, his partner abducted Gauri.'

Tara pondered over what Arun had said. 'Kajri, the Mehtas' maid, too mentioned a young man Naina had met a few times on the tram on her way to school. Is this the guy who was outside Gauri's house too? Was he working with another man? Could it be they together abducted the girls?'

Before Arun could answer her many questions, Mohan's voice floated in from the passage. 'Radha maasi, I hope Baabuji remembered to tell you about the prince and princess of Jaiwar coming home for dinner tonight.'

Mukund and Mohan entered the room.

'Whom do we have here, sister?' asked Mohan, summarily assessing Arun, his uniform and posture.

'This is Inspector Rao of the Bombay Police and I have offered to help him with his enquiries regarding the disappearance of the girls,' said Tara.

'Mrs Sethia had some theories which she has shared with me. I am thankful for her co-operation. I doubt there is anything else to add to them, going forward. I suppose I should take your leave and let you have your lunch,' said Arun, standing up to leave.

Mukund, who had also arrived for lunch, noticed the fleeting look of annoyance pass over Tara's face and realized his sister was displeased with the dismissal. Her intelligence and keenness were often dismissed due to her gender.

'Rao sahib, I suppose you aren't too busy to have lunch with us. It would give Mohan and me a chance to know more about our city and the work you do to keep it safe.'

Arun was not too keen to accept the offer, but after a bit of cajoling, he reluctantly accepted and the group proceeded to the dining room.

Radha had ensured the table was set for six and that everything was in place for their guest too. When Moolchand entered the dining room, he saw Inspector Rao seated at the table. 'What a surprise it is to meet you here, Inspector Rao! It has been a while since we last met.'

'Moolchandjee, the pleasure is mine,' said Arun, standing up and folding his palms in the customary Hindoo greeting. 'It has been a while since we met at the reformist meeting in Poona. If I am not mistaken, that was way back in 1896,' said Arun, glancing slyly at Tara, before taking his seat. Tara was astounded. He knew all along who her father was. *Why the elaborate ruse then?* she wondered. But she wasn't complaining.

The lunch was a relatively quick and an engaging affair with the men talking about the reformist movements, Bombay still reeling from the plague of last year, an increasing crime rate and unrest among the residents of the city. Finally, as the men started to retire to the living room, Mukund asked, 'Rao sahib, any lead on the missing girls' case?'

'A body was found,' Arun and Tara answered in unison.

Their interest piqued by this latest development, the men wanted to know more.

'While I don't have the liberty to discuss the case with anyone, your daughter was present when we broke the news to the family. We have identified the body as that of Naina Mehta. We have kept the identities of the girls a secret so far. We don't want the press to know anything till we are ready with a statement. The families don't want anything to be made public owing to the shame and taboo attached. Come to think of it, how on earth did you figure out who the girls were, Mrs Sethia?'

Tara blushed at the direct question and five pairs of eyes looking at her earnestly. 'Well, I knew the girls were from Ratanbai School and all I had to do was visit the school, which I did this morning. I garnered my information when I was there. Since then, I have visited the homes of two of the girls and that is where I met Inspector Rao.'

Arun was again impressed with the way her mind worked. 'I hope Mrs Maneckjee did not share this information with you. She was sworn to secrecy.'

'Please don't be upset with her. She was truly stressed and wanted to know my opinion on how this situation could be handled. My primary reason for the visit to the school today was to discuss a scholarship that I plan to set up for educating girls. We, however, did discuss the case and how the missing girls had caused bad publicity for the school. She was worried about parents of the other girls withdrawing their wards. To top it all, there is talk of the orthodox sections of society planning a protest. As it is, women's education is at its nascent stage and such incidents don't help its case,' concluded Tara.

'How have Kalyanjee bhai and Gangaben taken to the news?' enquired Radha. 'They must be devastated to know their daughter is never to return.'

'Not too well. Naina was to get married on the return of her betrothed from Lahore. He was to join the family business upon his return and they were to wed post that. It is indeed a very trying time for the family,' said a solemn Tara.

She knew what it meant for parents to lose their child. She had witnessed the devastation Jivan's death brought on his parents.

Deciding to gather more information from this highly connected family, Arun changed the conversation. 'How is your family connected to the royal family of Jaiwar? I overheard you are having them over for dinner tonight.'

'The Raje of Jaiwar and I have been acquainted for a long time.' Moolchand answered. 'Our fathers were friends. During the Uprising of 1857, the current Raje and his siblings sought shelter at our home in Baroda. Since then, the families have kept in touch, meeting at various occasions. Now with the prince moving to Bombay, we hope to keep in touch more often. Why do you ask, inspector?'

Just then Shankar entered the room with more news, 'Sir, Constable Wagh has sent a messenger. Mehtajee and he will meet you at the morgue shortly. Is there anything I can help with, Inspector sahib?'

Arun nodded his thanks and stood up to leave. With folded hands, he said, 'Thank you for having me over for lunch. It's been a privilege to dine with you and your family, Moolchandjee.'

'It is nice to see a young man such as you take a path that is riddled with challenges. I am sure your parents would be proud of you,' said Moolchand, bidding the detective farewell.

Arun nodded solemnly and walked out wondering if at all his father would approve of him and his 'path'.

~

Dr Webb and Arun awaited the arrival of Wagh and Mehta to identify the body at the former's office. Upon their arrival, Arun was surprised to see Ganga along with Kalyanjee. The parents were visibly shattered on seeing Naina's body. Arrangements were being made for the release of the body so that they could conduct the last rites.

Wagh was consoling Kalyanjee, while Arun waited with a sobbing Ganga and a sombre Kajri, who had come along with the Mehtas. Remembering Tara's words, Arun motioned for Dr Webb's assistant to stay with Ganga while asking Kajri to step out for a conversation.

'Kajri, do you remember the man Naina spoke with frequently?' asked Arun.

'What man, sarkar? I have no idea what you are talking about?' replied a nervous Kajri.

'If you think you can get away with lying to a police officer, you are wrong,' Arun countered. 'I have it from a number of sources that you are aware of the young man who met Naina on the tram. Do you remember his face? Your answer could help us identify a suspect. Don't you want to see Naina's killer punished?'

Kajri nodded shamefaced. Arun showed her the sketch of the person who was seen outside Gauri's house. Kajri exclaimed, 'Yes, it seems to be the same person Naina bibi used to talk to on the tram! He looked decent and used to say that he was going to be a doctor. Though I never got his name. Do you think he could be the killer, sahib?'

'I cannot answer that at present,' said Arun, folding the sketch. 'But thank you, Kajri. You have indeed been of help. If you were to remember anything else about this person or any of their conversations, do inform us.'

Dr Webb and Kalyanjee stepped out with an inconsolable Ganga. The last rites would be performed once everyone including Naina's fiancé and family were notified and till then Dr Webb offered to keep the body in an ice box to slow its decomposition. Although reluctant, the Mehtas agreed to the suggestion. Being in water for a considerable time had already speeded the decomposition process and they hoped they could preserve their daughter's identity and dignity a bit longer.

Arun and Wagh walked towards the station.

'Sahib, if the boy seen outside Gauri's house is the one Naina spoke to, does it mean he is connected to both girls in some way?' Wagh asked on their way. 'What about the third girl? How is he connected to her disappearance? Do you want me to put my khabris on his tail?'

Arun nodded his assent and set about piecing all the information he had so far.

five

These foolish men had picked the wrong girl. But then it was alright. They would exchange the other one in place of the one who died. They would bear the loss. As for the wrong one, a new buyer will be found soon. A new plan was set in motion. The usual parties would have received the letters. Soon, there will be a buyer and this time nothing will go wrong.

7 June

Arun had a note waiting for him on his arrival in office. It was a dinner invitation for the next day from his aunt. She was upset that Arun had not found the time to visit them yet. Arun sighed, considering he had a crime to solve and definitely no time to socialize. But saying no was not an option either.

Arun's office, while airy and bright, did not yet have everything he needed. A huge writing desk occupied the far end of the room while a small seating arrangement was in place for visitors near the window complete with Chippendale chairs. Arun sometimes missed his Poona office for all the touches he had made to make it his own.

Arun liked to place all his thoughts and timelines of a case in a structured manner. Using a piece of charcoal, he set out to write down the timelines, theories and suspects on the floor behind his desk. In his Poona unit, he did so, on a blackboard, however space was a constraint here and he had to make do with whatever he had.

A sudden commotion outside his office distracted him, but Arun continued to jot down the points and focus his thoughts. The booming voice of Deputy Thakore from outside caught his attention. He stood up, dusted off his trousers and turned to see a surprised Thakore, a flustered Wagh and a vexed youth standing in his room, all staring at him and his writing preference.

'What can I do for you, gentlemen?' asked Arun, calmly wiping his hands on a handkerchief. Thakore was the first to recover from the unexpected scene. 'Rao, whatever for are you scribbling on the floor! Wagh, ensure the inspector gets a decent blackboard in his office at the soonest.'

'Yes, Sir,' replied Wagh. 'Also, inspector, this man here claims he has news on the abducting case. I have been trying to tell him that he can share his details with me, but he is hell-bent on meeting you.'

'All this commotion has brought me to you, Rao. As for you, young man, introduce yourself and tell us why you think you have information regarding the abduction,' commanded Thakore.

'I am Omkar Sawant. Vidya Damodar Naik, the missing girl, and I are engaged.'

It was late afternoon. Radha and the rest of the household were frantically making arrangements for dinner and there was a lot of activity going on in the kitchen when Tara walked in. She stood in a corner and observed all the chaos, the cause of which was still funny to her. Radha spotted her and walked up to have a word with her. 'How is it that your father invites royalty and just forgets to mention that they are coming over for dinner? Bless Mohan to let me know. You understand there is so much to do,' she said in a flustered tone. 'Everything needs to be perfect for royalty. However are we to get dinner ready at such short notice?'

'Calm down, Radha maasi. You have known the prince and his family for a long time. I am sure they won't be too fussy. Let's be practical. Now don't waste time arguing with me. Just tell me how I can help and let's get to work.'

Ushering Omkar into his office, Arun motioned him and Thakore to be seated at the chairs by the window.

'Tell us everything from the beginning, young man,' motioned Thakore.

Omkar looked troubled and Arun decided the situation needed a calm treatment.

'Omkar,' pacified Arun, 'we understand your distress and want to help you. If you could tell us all the facts, we can get Vidya back at the soonest.'

Omkar looked up and quietly handed a note to Arun and began his tale. 'I am a civil servant, a clerk at the municipal corporation. Our families hail from Konkan and had arranged our marriage when we were both children. Although my family is wealthy and I really don't need to work, I wanted to be a self-made man.'

Arun looked on sympathetically.

'I also desired my bride to be educated and old enough to be my partner in the truest sense. Thankfully, my parents agreed to this and Vidya continued with her schooling.'

'What about Vidya's family? Are they rich too?' enquired Thakore.

'Vidya's father is with the Treasury and he moved from Konkan to Bombay just over a year ago. They don't have a lot of land or heirdom to support them financially. My future father-in-law Naikjee's, job is their only steady income apart from some farmland back in their hometown. Vidya and I had not seen each other in the last five years. We met just over three months ago at a family dinner. Since then we have been meeting often, especially during my lunch break. I felt it would be nice to know more about each other before we actually got married. We both enjoyed this courtship. Apart from her friend, who accompanied us, no one else knew about our arrangement.'

'When did you get to know of the abduction and why were you contacted instead of the parents?' enquired Arun.

'I am unsure why I have been contacted. I was to meet Vidya after school, during my lunch hour. Our arrangement was to meet on Tuesdays and Fridays at 1.00 p.m. I then accompanied her and her friend home before returning to work. I was running late yesterday and when I reached our spot, Vidya wasn't there. I waited for her for another ten minutes before heading back to work. I assumed she couldn't make it and did not have enough time to let me know.'

Gathering his thoughts, he continued, 'I was invited for dinner at her place that evening. It was on arriving there that her parents confessed about her abduction and the police complaint that was lodged. I was too shocked to react. Her family is completely at a loss. I couldn't confide in them about our meetings. I received this strange note a short while ago at my place of work. It was left on my desk and I knew it was Vidya it spoke about. I had to do something. Please help me.'

Arun asked for the note. Omkar placed it on Arun's desk for Wagh and Thakore to also read it.

I KNOW WHERE SHE IS. YOU HAVE 4 HOURS TO DECIDE IF YOU WANT MY HELP OR NOT. IF YOU WANT TO SAVE HER, TIE A WHITE CLOTH ON THE WINDOW OF YOUR HOME.

The note was in block letters and written clearly to mask the identity of the writer. Arun contemplated this and then decided on a course of action. 'Tie the white cloth and inform us as soon as you hear from this person again. You and I are going to save Vidya.'

Omkar left, agreeing to inform the police on hearing from the mystery person.

'Wagh, what have you got for me on the mysterious young man?'

'Sir, the same person was spotted outside Gauri's house yesterday afternoon. By the time the servants could catch him, he had given them a slip. The informer outside the Deshmukh house managed to follow the man for a short distance before losing track of him. He said he took off eastwards and was last seen boarding a tram bound for the eastern godowns.'

'I believe the young man we are looking for resides in that part of the town. Check with the lodges and guest houses there if they know of him. Take the sketch of the man and also check with the hostels and chawls in the area. This man could be an accomplice, or not related at all. Either way, it is time we meet the only lead we have so far,' Arun instructed Wagh.

Arun turned to Thakore, 'Sir, I believe we may have someone who is troubled in his mind. But we need to check all possibilities before ruling anyone out. Meanwhile, I need your assistance.'

'Anything you need to close this case and catch the culprit. What have you in mind?'

The royal prince of Jaiwar, Jaswant Singhji Kaushal, popularly referred to as Yuvraj Jaswant, and his sister Shivani arrived promptly at 7.00 in the evening. They were both elegantly dressed—befitting royals but did not look too out of place either. Moolchand and his sons welcomed them. By the end of the evening, Shivani and Tara became fast friends. Jaswant noticed how Tara put his shy sister at ease and spoke with her on a varied range of subjects.

Suddenly, feeling Jaswant's gaze upon her, Tara turned and asked, 'Yuvraj, may I ask you something?'

'Yes, what is it that you want to know?' said a smiling Jaswant.

'Tell us more about Jaiwar. How was it growing up in a palace? Why did the family move out?'

'Jaiwar has been our seat for over 150 years. The Kaushals have been Raje ever since I remember. My grandfather built the extensions to the current palace. Our province has some of the best masons and we have been trading for genera—'

'Growing up in a big palace can be daunting at times,' Shivani interjected. 'But I have some fond memories of growing up in Jaiwar. It all changed the day after Diwali, about four years ago.'

Seeing the stricken expression on her face, Jaswant patted Shivani comfortingly and continued narrating the story.

'There was a fire at our palace. My parents and I were out in a neighbouring district for a celebration. On our way back, we saw the roof ablaze. My father and I reached the palace and found the entire village pitching in to put the fire out. A few did not make it alive of the inferno. The entire east wing was cordoned off and closed for investigation. Mother couldn't recover from the incident and Father decided to move the family to one of our estates in the hills while the palace was restored. After that, my business interests got me to Bombay. Shivani decided to join me a few weeks ago.'

'Post the move from Jaiwar, my education has been very intermittent, and Bhaiya here wanted me to continue my studies till my wedding. I plan to stay in Bombay till then,' Shivani pitched in.

An uncomfortable silence ensued.

'How do you find the city of Bombay, princess?' asked Moolchand, changing the topic. Subsequent conversations touched upon many general subjects.

'Maybe we could meet at my residence, Tara bai. You can come over sometime,' said Shivani as they were taking their leave. Tara accepted her invitation, glad to find company and a friend in Shivani. And strangely, she felt there was something more to the royals' presence than it seemed.

six

8 June

A rustling sound from the far left corner of the room had Vidya ready to scream. 'Hello, is anybody there?' whispered a weak voice. Vidya gulped and opened her mouth to reply. Her parched throat left her croaking out a rough 'yes'.

Vidya could hear some more rustling and then a matchbox being struck. A soft light flooded the otherwise dark room. In the faint candlelight, Vidya could see the other figure crawl towards her. Holding her breath, Vidya looked at the other person in surprise.

'It is me…Gauri,' whispered the other girl, placing the candle near the wall and settling next to Vidya. 'Looks like we are both trapped here.'

It was almost midnight when the royal guests took their leave. Tara later found her father by the veranda playing his ektara. Moolchand was indeed different from his contemporaries. During his trade journeys, he acquired many collectibles from foreign lands and added them to his daily routine. Music was his way of unwinding after a long day at work.

'Baabuji,' Tara said softly, standing at the doorway, 'are you aware of the full story of the fire?'

Moolchand continued playing for a couple of more minutes before he put the instrument aside and motioned his daughter to join him on the swing.

Once she was seated beside him, he asked, 'Tara, what is it that you seek? I have not seen you take such interest in anything ever since Jivan's death. What has caused this sudden transformation? Why are you so fascinated with crime now?'

Tara was at a loss for words. But she decided to bare her soul to him. 'Baabuji, Jivan and I shared everything. Ours was not the usual marriage, where the woman is considered a secondary citizen in her own home. Jivan loved me and respected my thoughts.'

Moolchand had always been in awe of his youngest child. Since childhood, she had a knack for ferreting information out of people. As she had grown up without a mother, Moolchand always indulged her. He also knew his daughter was very rational and could be depended on during a crisis. She was stubborn, but in a nice way. Perseverance wasn't a bad quality and Tara had a huge reserve of it. He however worried at times. *What if Tara's doggedness is misunderstood? What if it results in something worse?*

'When we were ambushed on our last travel together, Jivan and I were discussing his latest case. He was sure a prominent figure was involved and that some officials in the British government were in cahoots with him. Jivan had unearthed some clues and told me about writing to his superiors warning them of his suspicions. When the attack happened and I was thrown off the carriage, the last words I heard before Jivan was shot was, "You were warned to mind your business. Lala doesn't like loose ends." I even mentioned this to the police later. No amount of crying hoarse or pressure from the Sethias resulted in an investigation into the Lala's affairs. The police refused to listen to me and termed me a grief-stricken woman who didn't know what she was saying.

'Jivan never got the justice that he deserved. I was treated badly both by the law and society. I know as a widow they didn't expect me to speak out, but this was not a usual situation,' said an overwhelmed Tara.

She had never spoken about the days that followed Jivan's death and the turmoil she had been put through in the last two years.

'There is nothing usual about your situation, Tara,' her father said grimly. 'You are a widow, with an inheritance of her own. I got you back home, to save you from the clutches of Jivan's extended family as well as that of Lala maybe. As you know, Lala is a wolf in a sheep's clothing. On the one hand, he is a philanthropic businessman and on the other, his business is full of shady dealings.'

Tara nodded solemnly. She had always thanked her stars that her family had supported her regardless of the situation.

'Tara, they surely wanted you to live on in a controlled and suppressed environment. I am not sure what Lala's reaction would have been though. He may not have wanted any loose ends and you may have been endangered. All that is in the past now. Lucky for you, the barbers of Bombay decided to strike and come up with their own rule of refusing to tonsure widows. We are living in very uncertain times and things are changing rapidly, but that doesn't mean we disregard social customs and embark on a journey completely unknown.'

'I appreciate all that you have done for me, Baabuji. I am indeed fortunate that I did not have to forego my hair, colourful clothes, inheritance and dignity. After Jivan's death, my life went into a state of limbo. I had no direction or motivation. However, over the last few months, I have been trying to bring my life back on track and put the opportunities that I have to use.'

'Is that what you have been doing in your room all afternoon? Scribbling away about how you want to change your life? Don't try to deny it,' said Moolchand when Tara was about to protest, 'I am the still the one who settles the bills for ink and paper in this household.'

Standing up, Tara walked away from her father. 'I am not denying anything, Baabuji. I have indeed used up quite a few bundles of paper. Now I have decided to help those in need. Be it monetary help or otherwise. I won't deny that I promised

Mrs Maneckjee of my assistance in assuring the concerned parents of those missing. If I can in any way help them find justice for their dead and missing children, it would redeem the more unpalatable aspects of my life. My chance encounter with the inspector and seeing Naina's parents just fuelled my urge to help them get closure. If you feel I shouldn't involve myself, I will step back. Believe me, Baabuji, I only want to help, not cause any pain or bring shame to our family.'

Moolchand contemplated on what his youngest child had just told him. As a father, he was a little hesitant to let his daughter get involved in situations closely related to crime. But on the other hand, his daughter was rediscovering life and he didn't have the heart to push her back to a life he had rescued her from.

'Tara, I am glad you decided to share your feelings with me. I also approve of you helping others who could do with your help and understanding.'

'Oh Baabuji, I am so relieved! Thank you so much.'

'Just remember,' cautioned Moolchand, 'getting too involved with crime is not something I approve of. Try to stay away from it.'

Tara nodded her acquiescence. 'Now will you tell me what happened to Raje of Jaiwar's family after the fire?' she asked impishly.

seven

8 June

Arun's uncle Shrikanth Rao Agashe worked at the Treasury and lived with his wife Mina and their family in a good-sized house in the upmarket area of Gamdevi, outside the confines of the crowded Fort area. Arun had hoped that dinner with his family would bring some respite from the long horrid day.

Arun had a rather disappointing start as there were no updates from Omkar on the note. Wagh had been relentlessly pursuing the mystery man and his whereabouts, but with no luck. Thakore had informed Arun of Inspector Verma from the Central Provinces being out on a case. The files for the Jaiwar fire and other missing girls were not going to turn up anytime soon.

Dr Webb had sent his reports of the post-mortem. Suicide was ruled out. The girl had sustained injuries at the back of her head and there were rope marks on her wrists. Murder was suspected. Dr Webb also sent new evidence that he had found clutched in the dead girl's palms, a piece of cloth with an incomplete symbol. It looked like a kind of cloth used to pack things in before shipping them. Only a part of the symbol was now visible, owing to Naina's body being in water for a long time. Arun enlisted Kareem, one of his other constables, to dig up more information on this symbol.

To add to his frustrations, Arun read two articles in *The Times* on the ongoing case. He sure was intrigued by T.S. Dave's piece, which was in the Perspective section. Dave had outlined all the facts of the case—some known to the public, some unknown—

yet true as far as the police were concerned. The piece was well structured and many relevant questions were raised. The fact that Dave could look at the ongoing investigation objectively was obvious from the first read itself. *Where did this man get this information from? It is an article that warrants a reread*, thought Arun to himself.

The other article, which was extremely provoking even though it was based on known facts, was an unsettling read. Arun hoped the newspapers wouldn't print stories that could lead to untimely protests and unrest among the general public. He pitied the parents of the girls.

'Arun anna, this is my wife Manjula,' said Krishna, introducing his young wife. Krishna, the older of Arun's cousins, had married a few months ago. His was an unusual marriage. In an era of arranged and socially binding marriages, Krishna had totally gone with love. Arun exchanged pleasantries with the bride. Manjula, although extremely striking and well boned, was demurely dressed and had a pleasing personality.

The evening was spent laughing and knowing more about each other's day and his aunt's attempts at matchmaking for their teenaged daughter, Uma. Arun noted that his cousin's wife seemed to be well read and could contribute to conversations including economics and politics. Arun wished his own family was so open and informal with each other. After dinner, the men gathered in the veranda for a chat.

'How have you been, Arun? Are you in touch with your family back home?' asked Shrikanth.

'Uday anna regularly writes to update me on the estate and Venugiri. Amma usually sends her blessings and pleas for me to return to Venugiri through letters. Gayathri is busy with her children and family and I occasionally get a letter or two from her. You are aware, Baba hasn't spoken to me since that fateful day.'

'I understand, Arun. It must be painful for you to not meet

your family. I remember Anna was not very pleased with me joining the Treasury either; however with the bulk of the estate going to him, he knew I had to earn money and couldn't order me to stick around. As for Sumitra, I haven't seen my sister after the day you left to join the police academy.'

A short spell of silence descended as both men contemplated their shared past.

'Krishna, how did Manjula and you meet? I hear she isn't from our part of the country. Do tell more on the romance,' said Arun playfully.

Krishna blushed a little. 'Manjula and I met when I was working at a cotton mill near Baroda as an accountant. My family was visiting Baroda during the Navaratri festival as Uma and Amma were keen to soak in the festivities. During their visit, we were invited by Gehlotji, the royal treasurer of Baroda. It was at their place that I first met Manjula.'

Just then Manjula entered carrying sugarcane juice for the men, disrupting the conversation. 'Uma will get the paan in a few minutes,' she said, placing the tray on the table.

The men talked for a few minutes on other happenings and then turned to the case.

'Are you investigating the missing girls' case, Arun? Any luck with the culprit?' asked Shrikanth.

'It is not a very straightforward case. Each day is a challenge and we are running out of time.'

'I am thinking about the families of the girls. How awful for them. How do you handle them, Arun anna?' Krishna asked.

Uma entered with paan and placed the box on the table.

'It is difficult,' Arun continued. 'And it has only gotten worse. The case is no longer just of abduction. One of the girls was found murdered this morning.'

There was pin-drop silence in the room and a look of shock on everyone's faces. Arun realized his folly. These were just ordinary people who did not witness crime daily and could be shocked easily. Uma particularly looked extremely pale.

'Please forgive me, Uma. Do take a seat. You look like you can do with a glass of juice yourself,' said Arun, handing her a glass from the tray.

Manjula sat next to her sister-in-law and tried to calm her down. Mina entered at that moment. 'Whatever did happen here? Uma is scared like a drowning kitten,' admonished his aunt.

'We were simply discussing the missing girls' case,' said Krishna, pacifying his mother.

Arun noticed that Uma had recovered from the initial shock. She however looked extremely uncomfortable, as if she wanted to say something.

To avoid any unpleasantness, Arun apologized again and decided to take their leave. His aunt and uncle came till the door to see him off. 'Do visit us again, Arun. We have missed meeting you during our annual family gathering in Venugiri,' said Srikanth. Promising them of a longer visit as soon as the case was solved, Arun left.

eight

8 June

Vidya and Gauri brainstormed and plotted ways to escape their predicament. They stopped briefly only to hurriedly gobble up a small lunch of rice and some insipid dal. Their lunch was pushed into the dark room via a small opening at the bottom of the big iron door. The only way of knowing the time was through the two high windows on either side of the stone room. At times, the sound of waves crashing against the rocks felt quite near and sometimes, it was a soft lulling sound.

'How I wish we knew where we are!' grumbled Gauri. Vidya and Gauri were both exhausted and knew it was late at night. The birds had stopped chirping and the noise of the bustling city had died down. Moonlight streamed in through one of the windows.

'The tide is picking up again,' said Vidya. Gauri gave her a bland look. 'We are definitely somewhere very close to the open sea. It could be the docks. Maybe we are in a godown.'

'No, this cannot be a godown. The ones near the dock have sunlit roofs and no windows. This structure is made of stone. The newer ones with windows and sunlit roofs are a mix of stones and cement,' said Gauri.

'How would you know for sure?' countered Vidya.

'Because Baba just rented one of the new godowns to store his wares when they arrive by boat or have to be shipped out. We had all visited the godown then,' answered Gauri smugly.

'Then, it only leaves us with one possible option. We are definitely being held prisoners at the old lighthouse at Colaba Bay.'

The girls fell silent. They could both hear the lapping of the waves against the rocks outside.

They had met late last night at the rendezvous spot. His partner was excited and brimming with grand plans. They discussed the next steps. It was agreed he would keep an eye out for the perfect opportunity, while the partner handled the logistical end of things.

The problem of finding a new girl was solved. He chuckled to himself thinking about his partner's situation. Poor man, he had no idea what was in store for him!

'I am so close to victory, I can almost smell it'.

When Arun reached his lodging in the evening, he found that Omkar's note had come in. It stated a time and place for the rendezvous. The meeting was scheduled at the godowns near the docks for 4.00 the next morning. Arun looked at the wall clock. It was 10.00. He dashed off a note to Wagh and Omkar asking them to meet him at the docks at 3.00 in the morning. He wanted to ensure everything went as planned.

As a precaution, Arun decided to enlist Inspector Shukla's help. He sent an errand boy employed by his landlord with a note to Shukla asking him to be ready to be picked up at 2.30 a.m. for a rendezvous with an informer.

So far, the crimes seemed like a straightforward case of abduction. However, the new developments—of Naina's murder and the lack of a ransom demand—definitely made it all the more complex. There were some observations he wanted to discuss with Shukla and get his opinion on.

Inspector Shukla was surprised to see a boy waiting at his lodgings with Arun's note. Hurriedly, he scribbled a reply and sent the boy back with it. As was decided, Arun came to pick Shukla up at his guest house sharp at 2.30 in the morning and together, they set out for the docks. Omkar and Wagh were already waiting for them there by the time they reached.

'Inspector Rao, you did not tell me there were others involved!' Shukla asked, a little surprised.

'Shuklajee, meet Constable Santosh Wagh. And this young chap here, Omkar, is the one who has been contacted by the informer. They are slated to meet at 4 a.m.'

The four of them discussed the plan. Arun, Shukla and Wagh would be a few meters away, hiding behind the crates near the outer buildings while Omkar waited at the designated spot for the informer. As soon as Omkar and the informer met, the police would nab him and take him in for questioning. It was a straightforward plan.

The trio took their place and eagerly awaited the arrival of the informer. Just before 4 a.m., they were distracted by a flurry of activity on the shoreline. Wagh realized it was time the fishermen set sail from the docks to bring in the morning catch. He quietly tiptoed to where Arun was hiding and explained the situation to him.

The clock tower struck 4.00. Omkar was waiting amidst the growing crowd looking for his informer. Every once in a while, he turned around to ensure the police had him in their range of vision.

Amidst the frenzied activity, someone suddenly pushed Omkar and he fell towards the water crying out for help. Arun, Shukla and Wagh rushed towards a falling Omkar. Shukla was the first to reach Omkar, who luckily was holding onto one of the cleats. 'Are you hurt, young man?' he queried.

'I am fine. Somebody pushed me. I had no time to break my fall or look at the person.'

A crowd started to gather around the men. Wagh set about assuring everyone and asking them to disperse. Arun looked around trying to gauge who could have been the informer. Turning back, he noticed a piece of paper lying near one of the cleats. Picking it up, he quickly tucked it into his pocket. He knew they could not afford to lose another chance to nab the informer, or maybe the culprit himself. This person was smart enough to spot them. How else could he have known about the plan? He had to take charge of the situation even if it meant hiding a crucial detail about the case from the others for now.

It was decided Wagh would take Omkar home. Arun and Shukla went their way, agreeing to meet later in the morning at the police station.

nine

9 June

Tara was ushered into the drawing room of the Jaiwar house. Shivani came in dressed as royally as ever making Tara cringe at her own simple attire.

'How nice of you to come calling, Tara bai!' greeted Shivani. 'Bhaiya is out at the moment, we can however talk over tea.'

Over tea, Shivani asked Tara about her childhood and growing up in Bombay. The two ladies chatted lively when Tara heard the clock strike 11.00.

'Shivani, I was wondering if you would like to go on a ride with me to the Hanging Gardens and take in the view of the bay. The view of Bombay Harbour is stunning from there. We can do a quick picnic and then ride along the sea face.'

Shivani was thrilled at the prospect of a picnic. Growing up in a royal household meant adhering to strict protocols and picnic with non-royals wasn't an everyday occurrence. Shivani wanted to make the most of her new-found freedom.

'Have you seen the new hotel that is being built along Apollo Bunder? I have heard it offers a beautiful view of the sea,' said Shivani excitedly as they both boarded the carriage.

Thus Shivani and Tara set out to take in the sites of the ever-growing city of Bombay and walk along the manicured lawns of the Hanging Gardens. Tara had sent a note to Shivani the day before asking for a mid-morning meeting. She wanted to befriend the young girl and at the same time hoped to get some more information about Jaiwar and the palace fire as well. In fact, she had asked Radha to pack a small picnic hamper that Shankar now carried for them. Shankar was also entrusted with the job of ferreting out information from the local fishermen and shop owners once they reached the sea face.

'How are you finding the city, Shivani? Have you enrolled yourself in a school already?'

'The city is so vibrant. I have met so many people from such diverse professions. Sadly, I was not aware that there is so much to learn. I don't have much time left.'

'You are just 13, what is the hurry?'

'Do you mind if we sit for a while, Tara bai?' said Shivani, a little tired.

They decided on a spot under a banyan tree and Shankar laid out the picnic fare. 'My father has confirmed my alliance with a royal family of Saurashtra. We will wed after my 14th birthday. So you see, I just have a year to learn everything I want to, be it in terms of modern subjects or the way a royal princess needs to conduct herself and see places. I really don't know what is in store for me once I marry.'

Although Tara knew she was nobody to dissuade Shivani from marrying so early, she sincerely hoped her future husband would not mind if she continued studying.

'Have you met your betrothed? Maybe he won't have any objection to you continuing with your studies after marriage,' suggested Tara.

Shivani shook her head. 'I haven't met Mahendraji yet. I will be meeting him at the royal feast his family is hosting to announce the engagement. Jaswant bhaiya told me he is educated and has great ideas when it comes to introducing reforms in his principality. The people like him and look forward to his reign. That may be the case as an administrator. I do not know if that will be the case as a husband as well.'

After a moment of silent contemplation, Tara spoke.

'Jivan, my husband, was studying to be a lawyer when we first met. His family has business investments with mills and they also have properties spread across the state of Baroda. Jivan always wanted to study law and be a successful lawyer. He wanted to help people. In fact, by the time we were married, I was aware of all the cases he was dealing with and he always sought my opinion in some tough scenarios. Our relationship blossomed due to mutual respect, love and a great friendship.'

Shivani tried to assimilate what Tara was trying to tell her. 'Shivani, I am not sure how much older Mahendraji is than you, but if you want to play an important role in his life, don't let fear govern your thoughts or actions. You seem to be a sensible girl and any man would be honoured and lucky to have you beside him. We are heading towards a new century, a new dawn. As a woman and a future queen, you will need to take decisions that will propel your subjects towards development and growth. I am certain that you will navigate your household and royal duties very well.'

'Thank you, Tara bai, for guiding me. I sometimes miss having someone older and wiser to talk to.'

'You're welcome, Shivani. I promise whatever we discussed today or in the future will be held in strict confidence. Shall we head to the sea face now, before it gets too warm?'

The seaside esplanade was a popular place among both the Europeans and the locals. Tara and Shivani came across many English and European ladies and their servants walking on the esplanade. Tara even stopped a couple of times to introduce Shivani to a few English ladies of her acquaintance. She later told Shivani that being acquainted with these ladies would help her ease into Bombay's bustling high society.

They walked past Apollo Bunder, where a massive building was under construction. 'Isn't this is the new hotel that is being built? I have heard so much about it. Once ready, it will make such a magnificent structure, won't it?' asked an excited Shivani.

'It is the dream of a local Parsee gentleman. He wants to build a world-class hotel that is open to all. It will put some of the snooty European ones to shame. It sure will be grand from the looks of it.'

They discussed the latest happenings around European hotels that did not let Indians enter their premises and how this new one could be the answer to the collective insult. Tara and Shivani made plans of having tea in the hotel tea rooms once it opened to the public.

Tara kept the conversation going and Shivani was equally excited to pitch in. 'You are so full of life and information. You do remind me so much of Madhubala didi,' Shivani suddenly said.

'Who is Madhubala?' asked Tara.

'Madhubala was my older sister. We don't speak much about her. Father forbade us from mentioning her,' Shivani looked momentarily disconcerted.

'Why would he do such a thing? After all, she is your sister and his daughter. And why are you saying she *was* your sister? Where is she now?'

'She committed the unspeakable act of falling in love with a commoner. She was a princess and betrothed to a prince from another royal family. Yet, she decided to elope with her suitor during Diwali celebrations.'

Taking a deep breath, Shivani continued, 'On that fateful night, Father locked her up in the east tower of the palace to thwart her plans. He was told by the spy he had employed, about her assignation. She tried to free herself and, in the process, accidently set fire to the curtains in her room. That was how the fire started. By the time my parents returned from the festivities, it was too late.'

'I am sorry for your loss, Shivani.'

Shivani smiled a watery smile, 'Please don't mention this to Bhaiya. He already feels guilty about being at the festivities. He feels if he had been around, he could have averted the disaster and saved the lives of all those who perished in the tragic fire. He wanted to talk to Didi and maybe meet her suitor too. But Father refused to listen to any reasoning. He couldn't save Didi and his relationship with Father went downhill after that. That is the actual reason why Bhaiya shifted to Bombay.'

'Are you aware of the suitor? What happened to him?'

'I was only nine when this happened. Bhaiya and I never got to meet him. I think Bhaiya had his suspicions, however he never shared them with Ma or me.'

'I understand how difficult this must be for you. I am sorry to have opened old wounds.'

'No, I should be thanking you. I have had no one to speak to about this incident. I was considered a child and no one spoke to me. Mother was heartbroken and we never discussed Didi. Bhaiya doesn't encourage my questions. I witnessed the fire and the cries of those in the eastern tower. Today, I finally got to speak about that incident.'

Tara was at a loss for words. *This young girl has suffered so much at such a tender age.*

Just then, Shankar spotted them and came running. 'You won't believe the information I have acquired for you, Tara bibi!' he exclaimed. Tara discreetly signalled him to stop talking. She did not wish to upset Shivani any more.

'Shankar, please call for the tonga. We are heading home.'

'Will you join me for afternoon tea, Tara bai? I do have something to show you. Maybe you can help me understand it.'

'I would be honoured. Tea would be great!'

He watched her board the tonga. His partner was keen on getting her and had already set things in motion.

She was the key to making the new plan a success. She was young, of good stock and a suitable addition to the client's collection. She was unlike the other one. Nevertheless, she would be the final act to the drama that had been brewing for a while now. 'It is time for me to take charge and get rid of all the excess baggage I have been forced to carry along all these years.'

One slip had cost him thousands of rupees. But no more! This time, there would be no scope for error. *I will drop the curtain on this drama soon.*

9 June

Inspector Rao, Inspector Shukla and Constable Wagh were with Deputy Superintendent Thakore, explaining the events at the docks.

'Are you suggesting, Rao, that you had the man in your view and yet managed to let him slip past? What am I to tell the commissioner? He expects us to find the person responsible before it becomes too difficult to contain the news and the unease among the residents of the city.'

Arun was taken aback as he was not used to being reprimanded. 'I understand, Sir. We are doing our best. I have requested Inspector Shukla to assist me on this case as he is well informed about it and is prepared. We should be able to close this before Shuklajee returns to Indore...' he added.

'I certainly believe he is one of the fishermen,' Shukla intervened. 'Otherwise how would he know about the 4 a.m. rush at the docks? We should ideally start looking and enquiring in that area if anyone has noticed something fishy.'

Arun wasn't sure if the fishermen would have any motive in nabbing these girls or even have the experience to write notes of information, but they could be the first source of information. 'Can I entrust this task to you? My constables are at your service.

You may choose one to take along with you, Inspector Shukla,' said Arun.

'You can count on me, Inspector Rao. I will leave immediately,' saying this, Shukla left with Constable Kareem to speak to the fishermen and the locals living in the dock area.

'Rao, I also have some information,' started Thakore. 'Inspector Verma returned to Indore early this morning. He was keen on returning my call. He had a lot to add to what we already have on our case and Shukla's story.'

'I am glad you spoke with him, Sir.'

'Apparently he had his doubts regarding the fire at the palace too. He felt it was highly coincidental that the two events of abduction and fire took place in the same area and on the same evening.'

'Was there any evidence of a connection? Did the investigation shed any light?' asked Arun.

'He claims there were a few rumours and village talk of the crown prince being seen in the palace at the time of the fire when he was supposed to be with his parents in a nearby village. Since no witness came forward, the police couldn't proclaim the fire as deliberate. Nor could they pin the crime on Jaswant Kaushal. Eventually it was dismissed as an accident.'

Arun carefully took in all this information.

'That night, the princess of Jaiwar, Madhubala, also perished in the fire. Most bodies were charred beyond recognition. It was a tough few weeks for the police department there...investigating a missing girl and a fire in the palace,' added Deputy Superintendent Thakore.

'Sir, if we assume the rumours point us in the right lines, then maybe the royal family itself was involved in either of the two crimes, or neither of them, or both.'

'This is a very interesting thought, Rao.'

Jaswant Singhji Kaushal is in town with his younger sister. Could there really be a connection to our case of missing girls? wondered Thakore.

9 June

Tea was a quiet affair, with both ladies nibbling at the snacks that accompanied the tea.

'Shall we retire to the upper lounge? I would like to show you something,' said Shivani.

Tara and Shivani retired to the upper lounge and Shivani fetched a small wooden chest with intricate carvings on it. Opening the chest, she lifted the section with all the jewellery and slid back a secret panel underneath it, pulling out a wad of letters.

'These are letters the suitor had written to Didi. There is also a letter to Jaswant bhaiya from Didi asking for his help.'

Tara picked up one of the letters and started reading it. 'But it is incomplete, Shivani…' she asked, confused.

'I am aware. Hence when our nanny's son found these among her belongings, he gave it to me. He asked me to hand them over to Bhaiya. I did not however reveal it to my family. Bhaiya was upset and Mother was engulfed in grief. No one knows these exist. I, on the other hand, so want to know who it was that Didi loved, and what happened of him.'

Tara contemplated this piece of information and the wad of letters. Was the suitor aware of Madhubala losing her life in the fire? Where was he now? Why had he never come forward?

'May I read through these letters? The suitor could have mentioned something that would help us glean his identity. If we do find something, maybe Yuvraj Jaswant could do something about it. Maybe all of you could find answers about that night,' suggested Tara.

Nodding, Shivani wrapped the letters back in a handkerchief and handed the entire box to Tara. Bidding adieu to Shivani and thanking her for the wonderful day, Tara and Shankar set off for home in the tonga. 'Now tell me, Shankar, what did you find at the fishermen's quarters?'

Turning sideways on his seat, Shankar narrated his encounter. 'I went to the beach where Naina Mehta's body washed ashore. The night before the body was recovered was quite uneventful. As usual, the fishermen were on their boats waiting to catch the early morning tide.

'It was only around 3.00 in the morning when they heard shouts and cries for help coming from the lighthouse at the end of the harbour. A few of them immediately rushed towards the sound. They were positive there was more than one person. Although they followed the cries, when they reached the spot they found no one, except a few scuff marks on the road as if a struggle had taken place. The men had no clue what had transpired. After looking around a bit and finding no one or anything suspicious, they left to do their work. It was only upon their return from sea after the morning catch that they found the girl's body. The fishermen were worried they would be dragged into a tedious enquiry and did not volunteer to disclose this information.'

Tara tried to assimilate this new information. *Arun's theory that Naina was trying to escape her captor when she was killed might actually be true,* Tara thought to herself.

'Oh, I almost forgot! One of them mentioned that from the voices they heard, they figured there was more than one person and those men had an accent that wasn't local.'

'Shankar, as soon as we get home, I need you to do one more thing for me,' she said, the excitement palpable.

ten

10 June

Arun was ushered into the plush office of Jaswant Singhji Kaushal, Crown Prince of Jaiwar, in the heart of the business district. The royal family was a patron of the arts of their principality and undertook trade to generate income for their artisans. Housed in a building near the stock exchange—in the heart of Bombay's business district, the prince's office had access to the docks, godowns and important banks of Bombay. When Arun walked into the office, the prince was surrounded by his retinue of workers. He had a regal air about him and looked at ease amidst the ensuing chaos. The usher announced Arun's arrival. The prince was surprised to find a police officer at his doorstep.

'Please come in, Inspector. How may I assist you?'

'I am Inspector Arun Kumar Rao of the Bombay Police. I would appreciate a few minutes of your time to discuss a pressing matter.'

Jaswant's office was big and airy. It had a large ornate roll top desk that lent a sense of importance to an otherwise-bare office space. Another low Davenport-style desk stood near the other wall with an accountant scribbling into a ledger. Arun also noticed another man in the office. He was middle-aged, not very tall, but with an air of importance about him. He was wearing a simple turban with an ornate pin bearing the royal crest of Jaiwar holding it in place.

'In private, if you please,' added Arun.

Noticing that Arun was not going to budge from his request

of a private audience with the prince, the man looked visibly irked. Jaswant, realizing the silent war, turned to the man and whispered something in his ear.

'But, Yuvraj,' said the man, smiling charmingly. 'I highly doubt you should be talking to the police. They are all the same, always harassing you.'

'Please don't mind Puranikjee, Inspector. He is my manager, but has been with our family for a long time. Ever since he lost his son, he treats me as one and can be overprotective at times.'

Puranik gave Arun a tight smile.

'It is alright, Puranikjee. I would like to render any assistance the inspector seeks. Please don't worry too much. Just ensure everything is in order for the next shipment.'

Jaswant motioned for his accountant and manager to step out too and requested Arun to take a seat. Arun noticed that Puranik's behaviour had not changed. He was still irritated with Arun. *Maybe Yuvraj Jaswant does know something important about the case*, thought Arun. Ordering for some refreshments, Jaswant asked, 'What is it that you would like to discuss, Inspector?'

Noticing the calm demeanour of the prince, Arun decided to be forthright about the issue.

'I have been investigating a spate of recent abductions. Unfortunately, we found the body of one of the girls yesterday. I am working at gathering information that might help me save the other two before it is too late.'

Jaswant's affable smile wavered. Stress lines bracketed his otherwise wrinkle-free forehead. Nevertheless, his etiquette forced him to ask, 'What can I do to aid your investigation?'

'The girls I am searching for were abducted from a local native school. They are from well-to-do progressive families. They were abducted in carriages. No demand for ransom has been made yet, however as I said, we found one body yesterday. Does the abduction pattern sound familiar to you?' Arun paused. 'A few years ago, a girl disappeared in a similar fashion from your province. In fact, it has come to our notice that it was on the same day as that of the fire in your palace in Jaiwar.'

A look of despair passed over Jaswant's countenance. Continuing, Arun said, 'There are rumours even today, that you were involved in it. Some even saw you near the palace on the night of the fire when you were supposed to be with your parents in a village nearby. If I may be forthright, what is your connection to it, Yuvraj?'

Sighing deeply, Jaswant began to talk. 'That night is still imprinted in my mind. My name was dragged through the mud back then. I might as well come clean with you today.'

Arun leaned back in his seat, carefully taking in Jaswant's side of the story.

'On that unfortunate night, four years ago, our family lost not just a wing of the palace but also some very loyal servants. But above all, I lost my sister, Princess Madhubala.'

'I am sorry about your sister. Losing her must have been tragic.'

'Things changed overnight for our family. She wouldn't have been in the palace tower if it were not for my father's stubborn pride. You see, she was in love with a commoner. Our father was against this and to teach her a lesson had put her under house arrest. His one act of stubbornness cost the family a daughter.'

Sighing, Jaswant rose from his chair and walked to the window. 'I have no idea when or how the rumours began. I had just taken over the business. And that evening, after fighting to put the fire out, I was making sure our orders were completed and trade shipments had gone out in time. But soon the police were knocking on our door asking all sorts of questions. Father was angry and I was inexperienced to handle such a situation.'

Arun thought maybe he was wrong to suspect him of any ill doing, as the only thing Jaswant seemed to be hiding was grief.

Nevertheless, he didn't know Jaswant very well and could not give him a clean chit based on just his version of the story.

Arun rose and walked over to the window too. 'Thank you, Yuvraj, for sharing this with me. It is my duty to solve this crime and save the girls. The case in Jaiwar was similar and I have to investigate it. It was not my intention to rake up an old wound.' The prince nodded and Arun took his leave.

~

As Arun walked towards his office, preoccupied with the latest conversation, he noticed a group of upset constables waiting in the corridor. He could sense residual anger in the air. Constable Wagh approached Arun and quietly informed him that Deputy Superintendent Thakore wanted to see him.

'Arun!' bellowed Thakore, seeing Arun walk into his office. 'The commissioner is extremely displeased and is looking for results. With the flak the police have been receiving for mismanaging plague relief measures, I don't want us to contribute to the mess by not solving crimes. Our only solid lead, and this morning you managed to lose that one too.'

Arun, in his desperate effort to placate his senior, told him about his recent meeting with Jaswant. Thakore tried to assimilate the new piece in this complex jigsaw puzzle when Omkar walked in.

'Good morning, Omkar. Glad you came in. I have a few questions for you. Please take a seat.'

'Would you like to hear Omkar recount his end of this morning's encounter, Sir? Maybe a fresh perspective will help us all,' Arun enquired. A somewhat mollified Thakore nodded for Omkar to take a seat.

Arun took the chair near the window. He always felt energetic when seated by the window, with the cool sea breeze and the warm light flowing in.

'Do you remember anything about the man who pushed you

this morning? His voice, or hair, or the shape of his body, or what he was wearing, anything at all that can help us?' Arun asked.

Omkar set about thinking. 'As you know, it was still dark when we were at the docks. I was extremely nervous and the crowd was not helping matters. All I could make out before I fell was that he was young and certainly shorter than me. I couldn't see his face or clothes.'

'I found this piece of paper lying near one of the cleats during our encounter this morning. It has just two words written on it: *No police*.' Passing on the chit to Omkar, Arun observed his reaction.

A baffled Omkar shook his head and muttered, 'I did not tell anyone about my visit here.'

Thakore, on the other hand, looked up at Arun and asked, 'Why did you not mention the note earlier?'

'I was not sure how this note fit into the scheme of things and wanted to ascertain if Omkar was aware of someone noticing his movements or knew about the rendezvous.'

'What else can you remember of this morning's encounter, young man?'

'It's all blurry. Everything happened so quickly. Oh, I did smell a hint of jasmine though!'

Both Thakore and Arun looked at each other in surprise. This was an intriguing piece of information.

'Jasmine could definitely mean perfume. But it is usually a feminine scent,' inferred Thakore.

'The person who pushed me was definitely a man, Sir. No woman could have that much strength.'

Arun shook his head. 'As it was dark and you can't be absolutely sure, let us not discount that line of thought.'

'I hope we haven't blown our chance of rescuing Vidya. What do you want me to do, Rao sahib, if he were to contact me again? I am deeply worried for Vidya. I believe we should tell her family of these new developments in the case. They are sick with worry,' said Omkar, worried.

Arun agreed to update Vidya's family on the latest developments in the case.

~

'Do you have any idea why we have been abducted?' asked a scared Vidya.

'My father is rich. Maybe they have abducted me for money. They might let us go as soon as they receive the money,' replied a not-so-confident Gauri.

'My father isn't rich. He is a civil servant. He won't have money to save me.'

'From the silk jacket blouse you are wearing, it looks like he had enough money to pay for it. It is of the latest style and has embroidery on it.'

Vidya blushed profusely. 'The blouse isn't mine. A friend loaned it to me.'

~

Vidya Naik's parents were simple people. On reaching their home, Arun sent the police constable to fetch Damodar Naik, Vidya's father, from his workplace.

Omkar and Arun sat in a narrow wooden bench-style day bed that doubled up as a sofa in Vidya's living room. Modestly decorated, Vidya's mother had ensured their humble home was warm and welcoming. However, today the atmosphere was tense.

A sense of doom prevailed in the household. Mrs Naik, a simple lady, dressed in a cotton saree typical of the coastal towns of Deccan, stood wriggling her hands. Just then the door opened and Mr Naik walked in hurriedly, almost gasping for breath.

'Omkar, is everything alright?' he asked, anxious.

Arun stood up to let a flustered Naik take his seat. Damodar Naik was an unassuming man in his late thirties. Typical of a civil servant, he was dressed in a dull-brown full jacket paired with a plain cotton shirt and dhoti. He deposited his turban by the door when he came in.

'Damodar kaka, the inspector has some information regarding Vidya. I have been working with the police to help free Vidya.'

Damodar turned anxiously towards Arun, who proceeded to sit on a corner chair. He updated the concerned parents of the recent developments. The Naiks were very perturbed by the end of it all. The mother was trying her best to stem the tears now flowing freely. She was relieved that her daughter was still alive.

'I don't understand why anyone would abduct our daughter. I believe the other two girls hail from very wealthy families. I am a mere civil servant, living off my wages. What can I possibly have that could be of interest to them?' moaned Damodar.

'Why would they contact you, Omkar? Who is this person who has information about our Vidya?' asked Mrs Naik quietly.

Unable to give them any clear answers to put their mind at ease, Omkar simply shook his head in despair.

The strain of putting up a brave front was showing on their faces. The mother was sobbing quietly. Arun had to pacify and reassure them of the efforts of the constabulary.

'I assure you, Naikjee, we are doing our level best to find your daughter. I believe if we trace Vidya, we will be able to free Gauri too. Do you know if any of your daughter's friends might be able to shed some light on this case?'

'Vidya has very few friends. Her closest friend is Uma Agashe. She is the daughter of my husband's senior,' said the mother in between sobs.

Arun was surprised to hear this bit of information. He remembered his cousin, Uma's, discomfort during the case conversation when he had met her last. Now that she was so closely connected with the case, he realized he had to have a chat with her at the soonest.

Promising to update them as soon as he had any information, Arun hurried back to the station.

eleven

11 June

It was 3.00 in the afternoon. Tara was busy reading the letters she got from Shivani to see if anything strikes her as odd, when Shankar came in.

'Tara bibi, you were right! The school confirmed that the person in the sketch was a new clerk who worked with them. He left on Wednesday after school and hasn't come to work since. No one knows where he lives.'

'Well done, Shankar. I might need to meet the inspector tomorrow. I have a theory that I want to run past him.'

'Tara bibi, what do I tell Sahib, your father? He will be annoyed if I again take off from my usual work to accompany you,' lamented Shankar.

'Leave Baabuji to me. I'll explain my need for your assistance. I need to head to the Town Hall first thing tomorrow morning. I will take one of our closed horse carriages. If you can let the inspector know and get him to meet me at the Town Hall at the earliest convenient time, that would be great. I'll stay there till I have met him. You can return to work. That way Baabuji won't be too annoyed.'

Shankar nodded grudgingly.

'Thank you, Shankar.'

11 June

On reaching his office, Arun was surprised to find an old blackboard ready for use. Calling for Constable Wagh, he set about listing all the pieces of information, dates, names and possible theories in neat columns. It was gratifying to finally write his thoughts without worrying about it getting swiped clean.

'What do you think, Wagh? Do I have everything so far on the board? Am I missing anything?' Arun asked.

'The list seems confusing. There is the youth who was seen outside Gauri's home, his accomplice, the mystery letter-writer. You have now added an unknown person from the Jaiwar fire case and Yuvraj Jaswant Singhji Kaushal to the list. Sahib, there are too many suspects in this case.'

'The case is baffling, I agree. There are many hidden elements that have not yet come to the fore.'

'What could be the motive of the abductor? Is it personal vendetta or money or professional rivalry?' debated Constable Wagh.

'The Deshmukhs and Mehtas are wealthy, while the Naiks are salaried people. Neither of the rich men is in the same trade, nor is their social circle the same. The only thing that connects the three families is their daughters and the school they go to.'

'Could it be because they are progressive?' suggested Wagh. 'After all, they are educating their grown-up daughters and the girls aren't married yet,' said a slightly miffed Wagh.

While not always agreeing to the general sentiment of people, Wagh knew that it was important to adhere to social norms. 'The orthodox sections of the society are not too happy about the families that are educating their girls. They feel the family hierarchy will not remain the same. Could it be the work of some social vigilante who wants to teach them a lesson?'

'Why would a social vigilante commit murder, Wagh? A crime

of that proportion would attract attention and social backlash. Unless the person has the clout to get away with murder and is sure of it, he won't attempt anything like this.'

Maybe the Yuvraj of Jaiwar did not tell me the complete truth after all, thought Arun.

Just then, the phone on Arun's desk rang. The operator at the exchange said it was a trunk call from the Central Provinces. It was Inspector Verma on the line.

'Hello, Verma sahib, what have you got for me?'

'Inspector Rao, I have some additional information for you on the Jaiwar abduction case. There were several other girls who had gone missing from the Central Provinces for almost six months prior to the fire at the palace. I have sent you an express delivery listing the names of the girls and places they were abducted from. It should reach you by noon tomorrow.

'The case of the Jaiwar missing girl was prominent because it coincided with the fire. There were rumours and we kept an eye on the prince and happenings in the royal household. Everything seemed as usual. Nothing out of the ordinary happened in the period following the fire. The royal household was in mourning owing to the deaths. However, trade was as usual, and shipments were on schedule. The missing girl was never found, nor was her body recovered. We eventually shut the case when even after about three months of investigation we found nothing. Did Shukla not tell you this?'

Arun was surprised as Shuklajee had told him he was transferred after the incident and that was the reason, he did not have so much information on the case. *What is going on?*

'I am thankful to you for the information, Verma sahib. As Shuklajee said he was transferred after the fire and did not have all the information, we had to trouble you.'

'I am happy to help. If we can solve the case, nothing like it. As for Shukla, he was not transferred; in fact, if I remember right, he asked to be moved to Indore. I heard he had also been promoted to an inspector within a year of the move. Tell him I asked after him.'

Arun was astonished on hearing about Shukla's transfer and subsequent rise in rank. He wondered why Shukla withheld the circumstances surrounding his transfer. *Was there more to this story?* he wondered. *I am sure Shuklajee has his own reasons for not divulging the full story.*

'Verma sahib, I appreciate your help with our case. Have a good day!' thanked Arun filing all the information for rumination later.

'Wagh, we will receive the names of the missing girls from Inspector Verma tomorrow. We need to add those to all the information we already have. Hopefully a new picture with lesser holes will emerge.'

There was a knock on the door and Constable Chavan hurried in. 'Sahib, as instructed I was keeping an eye on Omkar's residence this morning. I saw this girl duck into his residence. She must have been in a hurry, because as she exited she dropped this handkerchief. I picked it up as I followed her, but she ran into the crowded market square and I lost her.'

A light waft of jasmine filled Arun's nostrils. 'Can you describe her?'

~

The silence in between the conversation was unnerving. 'I was abducted when I was on my way to meet my intended. What about you, when did they nab you?'

'They got me while I was on way back home from school. I so did not want to go to school. It is that obstinate husband-to-be of mine who wants me to study, just because he is studying to be a barrister,' said an exhausted Gauri.

'Do you know where the other girl is?' asked Vidya.

'Oh, is there another girl? I have been floating in and out of consciousness. So when I saw you, I assumed it was just you and me,' said a distracted Gauri.

'Well, I hope she escaped, considering we haven't heard or seen her with us here.'

The duo fell silent. As far as small talk between roommates went, this was the weirdest Vidya had ever had. *Oh, when will I see my parents, Omkar and Uma again?*

―

The police sniffing into matters is a little too deep for comfort. Something is not adding up. Who is it talking to the police? Is someone in the crew trying to rat me out?

This business is integral to bigger things. I have to figure out a way to put an end to this leak. If the modus operandi is to be revealed, all the hard work over the years will be futile. I cannot let this happen. Those girls need to be dispatched soon.

―

11 June

All the constables gathered in Arun's office. Arun was a bit unsettled that Inspector Shukla had sent him a note instead of coming in. He wondered what the reason could be for Shukla's absence. He read the note. It said:

Spoke with the fishermen. Nothing much to report. No one seems to have noticed anything of great value. They heard cries for help but did not see anyone. Will not come in today. Have a personal job to finish before I return to Indore tomorrow.

Well, the note doesn't explain everything. But then, I can't expect the same level of dedication from an officer who is technically on leave. After all, this is the Bombay Police's case, not his, thought Arun to himself.

'What do you have for me, Kareem? Did you find anything

useful during your enquires at the docks?' asked Arun, folding the note.

'Sahib, I spoke with quite a few of them. One of them mentioned talking to another man who he assumed works in the police department, an inspector perhaps, earlier in the day.'

Frowning in thought, Arun nodded to the constable to continue. 'When I visited the fishing village to see if I could assist Inspector Shukla, I did not find him there. I assumed he had returned to the station. I bumped into a fisherman who said he told this other person also about an out-of-town accent. I asked him if the accent of the other person questioning him was like the inspector's and he said no. He clarified that the other officer he spoke to had a local accent. I thanked him and got back here.'

Arun wondered if Tara continued her involvement with his case. *If she had...* Arun hid a smile that formed involuntarily. *The other person mistaken by the fishermen could have been Shankar. Tara had a lot to answer for, but not now.* 'Thank you, Kareem, for relaying this to me. I guess the inspector forgot to include it in his note.' *But why had Shukla missed mentioning the out-of-town accent in his note?*

'Kareem, keep your eyes and ears peeled to the ground. Wagh, keep up your search for a man with jasmine scent. Chavan, how did your enquiry on the half symbol go? Did you find anything?'

'No, Sir, not yet. The dock workers don't remember seeing anything like that. I am heading to the godown, maybe we can get some information there.'

'Good work, gentlemen. Any information, come to me at the earliest. I must now head to my uncle's. My cousin studies at the same school as the missing girls.'

11 June

That evening, the Desai family had an unexpected visitor—Jaswant.

'Yuvraj Jaswant, what brings you here this evening?' queried Moolchand, surprised.

'Please accept my apologies for dropping in unannounced. I was wondering if Tara bai would be free to accompany Shivani and me tomorrow morning to Lady Herbert's Academy.'

Lady Herbert's Academy was one of the well-known centres in the city for women's Western etiquette training. Most young Indian women from the royalty and those from the upper classes who aspired to be diplomats' wives enrolled at the finishing school to gain skills required to navigate the complex societal protocols of the Western society. Tara was surprised with the request considering Jaswant would have people to take care of such things.

'I could have sent someone along with a note. However, you are friends of the family and it would have been extremely impolite, Moolchandjee, of me to do so.'

'Don't overthink, Yuvraj. Please take a seat,' gestured Moolchand.

'I hear it is the best in the city and the most affluent families send their girls there to hone their social skills. Shivani would like to continue her formal education and I have already made arrangements for her to be home-schooled. I hear you attended Lady Herbert's Academy and know Lady Herbert personally,' finished Jaswant taking a seat.

Tara, though puzzled with the request, agreed to accompany them to the academy.

'My sister looks up to you as a friend and a guide. It would be an honour, Tara bai, if you could help her transition to this city life and the new challenges she is to face.'

'I would certainly like to help, Yuvraj. What time would you want me to be ready?'

'We will pick you up at nine tomorrow morning.'

༄

Arun was apprehensive about questioning his cousin. He was sure that Uma knew something that could prove useful in cracking this case. For him, solving this case was a duty. But this new information and the fact that maybe his cousin was somehow involved in this notorious episode, made it personal.

I have to capture Naina's killer and put all those responsible for the abduction behind bars.

When Arun reached his uncle's house, he was ushered in by his aunt. 'Twice in two days, you are all set to break your own record, Arun.'

'I am sorry to have come in unannounced, Kaki. I wish to have a word with Uma, if she is available. It is actually official business.'

'Is it? Have a seat, Arun. I will call her. She just got back from school and is in her room,' his aunt said, walking towards her daughter's room.

After a while, a scared Uma entered the living room with Manjula, her sister-in-law, in tow.

'Don't be scared, Uma,' said Arun softly, sensing his cousin's discomfort. 'I merely want to know a few things about your friend Vidya.'

Once the ladies settled in the sofa across him, Arun continued, 'Is it true that you were aware that she is the third girl to be snatched from school? Why did you not come forth with this information?'

'A… Anna,' she replied hesitantly after a few minutes. 'I was shocked to know that Vidya had been abducted. The other two girls were from rich business families. They did not care much for education. They were in school to please their fiancés or on their family's insistence. Vidya is a very clever girl, genuinely wanting to study, but doesn't hail from a rich family.'

'I had loaned her one of my expensive jackets to wear, as

she was to meet Omkar, her fiancé, later in the day, after school.' Glancing at her mother, Uma became aware of the disapproval on her parent's face.

On Arun's nod, she continued, 'Her parents are not aware that Omkar and Vidya meet often after school. He usually walked us both home before returning to work. I was unwell and did not attend school that day. The next day at school, I realized it was Vidya who had disappeared right after school. I often wonder if it was the wrong girl they got that day.'

'Don't berate yourself,' consoled Manjula. 'You had no idea Vidya would be abducted. And it is not necessary that it was a case of mistaken identity.'

'Did you go to Omkar's residence today, Uma?' Arun asked point-blank.

Mina and Manjula gasped at Arun's question. A shaken Uma nodded mutely. 'I wanted to talk to him, without alarming anyone. I felt if I were to tell him about me lending my clothes to Vidya, it might comfort him to know that perhaps Vidya was not the intended victim. But when I reached there, he wasn't home. I saw some unknown person trying to open his door. I left immediately. I wasn't sure if that person saw me.'

Arun raised his eyebrows. *Another unknown entity? So many suspects yet not one is in my custody for questioning.*

Mina was lecturing Uma on the pitfalls of trying to do foolish things. 'How did you dare go to an unmarried man's house, and that too unaccompanied?'

'Do you use a jasmine perfume?' Arun interjected, trying to put an end to his aunt's tirade.

Both younger ladies nodded affirmatively.

'I suggest you be careful, Uma. Kaki is right. It will be best if you don't venture out on your own without informing anyone. It is for your own safety. Till such time that we capture the culprits and get the girls to safety, stay alert.'

Manjula comforted a sobbing Uma. As Manjula looked up, a fleeting expression of confusion mingled with dread was reflected in her eyes. Arun wondered if this was the entire truth or were his cousins still hiding something.

'I will take your leave now, Kaki,' Arun said, getting up.

'Why don't you come back for dinner, Arun?'

'No, Kaki. Thank you very much for the offer. I will see you all soon. Good night.'

Constable Wagh ensured a new blackboard was delivered to Arun's quarters along with the day's post. It was waiting for him at his doorstep when he got back. Arun put up a small workspace near the window. His writing desk, with the day's post, was already positioned close to the window to allow for light and air. He then set out detailing everything including the new information he had received from Inspector Verma, Omkar, Jaswant and Tara over the last few days.

The case had developed into a complex puzzle, with new information and revelations, and no clear line of thought. Could it be that the fire and abduction were coincidental and the clues or suggestions were just to divert attention from the actual case in Bombay? Could the royals be related to the current case in any way? A seasoned police officer like Shukla had not mentioned the out-of-town accent in his note. Was it a slip or was there any other angle?

Arun started listing every piece of information and conversation he had had in a chronological order. Everything—from the dates of abduction, the information he had on the families of the other missing girls, the current case, the royal family and its trade patterns, the fire at the palace to the death of the Princess Madhubala. The first girl reported to be abducted was from Bhopal. After that, it was a series of reports on missing girls across the region and the most highlighted one was the one in Jaiwar on the day of the fire.

A pattern was emerging. Something, however, was still amiss. Either the prince was a good actor or in great trouble. Either way, Arun decided it was high time the prince and he had another chat.

Arun received another note late in the evening. It was in a vaguely familiar hand. *What does she have to say to me? After all, we are just mere acquaintances.* It said: *Meet me at the Town Hall tomorrow noon.*

twelve

12 June

'Good morning, Tara bai. Hope my brother and I are not imposing on you,' said Shivani, getting ready to head for Lady Herbert's Academy. The Kaushals had arrived on time to pick Tara up. The trio headed to the academy. Tara had instructed Shankar to have a carriage sent to Lady Herbert's directly after her noon appointment.

'It is not an imposition, Shivani. I would love to help you settle into your new life here in Bombay. The city can be a little overwhelming for someone unused to this kind of living.'

The young princess was fascinated with her surroundings and tried valiantly to curb her enthusiasm.

Turning to an absorbed Jaswant, Tara said, 'Yuvraj, you seem a little lost today. Hope all is well.'

'Well, nothing of major concern, Tara bai. Just worried about some business end of things.'

'How is the business faring? I hear the marble statues, fountains and fresco from Jaiwar are a big hit now. How exactly does it work at your end?'

'In recent years, the demand for our intricate work on stone has risen not only in India but across Europe too. With the opening of the Suez Canal twenty-nine years ago, trade had picked up. Father cultivated the right contacts in Europe and since taking over I have managed to grow it further.'

'That is really commendable. What kind of orders do you usually get?'

Jaswant relaxed a little once he started to talk about his business.

'It depends. Many European nobility and rich men who want to build extravagant homes place orders with us. We have diversified into creating intricate pieces that the ladies usually get excited about. In fact, as we speak, a new shipment is getting ready to sail. There is this marble inlay dressing table that an oil merchant in Aden has ordered for his third wife.'

'I never thought that royalty would step into the domains of trade,' teased Tara.

'We try not to let out into high society that the royal family is actively involved. I might not find the right wife if that happens,' said Jaswant jokingly. 'On a serious note, it is a wise financial decision that helps the province in many ways. Apart from contributing to the royal coffers, it also helps the regional artisans find a larger and more lucrative market. Everyone benefits. I have to thank Puranikjee, our manager, for having the forethought of using our own transport to move the goods. It saves a lot of trouble and money.'

'That is really thoughtful, Yuvraj! Look, we have reached the academy,' said Tara.

A set of new buyers has been arranged. The older one developed cold feet on hearing about the death of one of the missing girls.

Why do such feeble men exist? Here I am, racing against time and building an empire and then there are clients who are worse than a goat.

Time is running out. Someone is out to spoil his game. He has come too far ahead now to stop. His partner better buck up soon. This girl needed to be abducted before nightfall. To hell with their connections or lineage, if anyone were to double-cross him, they would have to pay for it with their life.

The day had not started well for Arun. On reaching the prince's office, he was informed of his unavailability. Puranikjee was courteous but firm that the inspector shouldn't wait for the prince, as he wasn't sure when he would return. Agreeing to inform him, he ushered Arun out.

So much for catching Jaswant unaware, mused Arun. Stepping out, he spied around a little. The office was in the better part of the business district and there was a lot happening. From people rushing to work, traders and businessmen arranging for goods to be picked up to the trams depositing more people by the hour, this was the hub of all activity in the city. *The prince has chosen the right place for his office.* Arun spotted a man selling mangoes across the street. Marching up to him, he bought a few, spoke with the seller a bit and boarded his carriage to head back to the station.

Constable Wagh was already in and Constable Kareem's and Chavan's reports were on his desk. Arun and Wagh were comparing notes when loud voices disturbed the discussion. Wagh stepped out to see what was happening. He returned with Kajri in tow.

'Sahib, Kajri has something she wants to tell us about our mystery man.'

Motioning Kajri to come in, Arun asked, 'What is it that you remembered, Kajri?'

'Sahib, I was with Naina bibi when we bumped into that young man, the one whose sketch you showed me. I only remembered this morning as I was cleaning Sethani's chamber that I had smelt jasmine oil on this man. It is unusual for men in Bombay to apply jasmine oil. They usually use coconut oil mixed with castor or sesame oil. I thought that could be useful and hence came in to let you know.'

Wagh and Arun looked at each other in amazement. 'That is excellent information, Kajri. You have indeed been helpful. Thank you. Have a good day. Wagh, please show Kajri out.'

Tara could sense many eyes on her. People were still not used to a woman being out in public and that too looking through old newspapers at the Town Hall. The staff at the Town Hall was puzzled at Tara's request, but she had work to do. She was also carrying the box of letters that Shivani had given her and was taking notes when she sensed a gaze on her. On turning around, she noticed Arun standing by one of the many pillars that dotted the big hall. She smiled and motioned him to come over.

She had chosen a desk in the corner of the hall with a big window. Sunlight poured in through it and one could have a good view of the activity on the main road. Many Englishwomen with their entourage could be spotted at Bombay Green, enjoying a breath of fresh air and plenty of shade in the park. Rechristened Elphinstone Circle in 1869 after the then governor Lord Elphinstone, the crescent of arcaded commercial buildings flanked by wide and tree-lined streets was set around the former Bombay Green and was considered the centrepiece of colonial urban planning for Bombay. Flanked by the Town Hall and Mint on the east and St Thomas Cathedral to the west, the erstwhile Bombay Green had been transformed from a dump of coconut shells to a very English streetscape. With the Mint right next door to the Town Hall, noon was always a busy time of the day, with most people stepping out for lunch.

Tara looked smart as usual. She was wearing a soft-pink sari with green and blue dots. Arun admired her for draping it in the old-fashioned dhoti style. In fact, it suited her. *Maybe her husband appreciates her dressing this way.*

'Why have you summoned me here, Mrs Sethia. In fact, I am amazed you are still involving yourself in this case,' said Arun, pulling up a chair next to hers.

'Rao sahib, keep your bias to yourself, especially when you are late for an appointment.'

'It is all because of that prince of yours,' grumbled Arun, instantly regretting mentioning the prince to Tara.

'You are investigating Prince Jaswant?' asked an astounded Tara. 'Why do you think he is involved?'

'I am still not completely sure how, but he is involved and I plan to pry it out of him.'

'Good luck with that! Although the prince did seem stressed this morning.'

Arun raised his eyebrows in silent enquiry.

'I accompanied him and Princess Shivani to Lady Herbert's today. Not that it is any of your concern.'

'So that is where he was this morning. Puranikjee could have mentioned that when I asked. What was there to hide?' muttered Arun, slightly irritated.

'In any case, let's not dilly-dally much. Come, take a look at what I have found. I am still not completely sure of my theory. However, I do have some other information that may come in handy,' said Tara.

Arun stood up to read what Tara was showing him. He noticed the staff and other readers looking at both of them oddly. He decided to ignore them and pay attention to Tara instead.

Arun and Tara scrutinized the newspaper clippings and notes that she had made.

'I recently discovered from Princess Shivani about the fire and how they lost the older daughter, Princess Madhubala, in it.'

'The princess was in love with a commoner,' added Arun, matter-of-factly.

Tara looked at him with raised eyebrows.

'You are not the only one sleuthing. I happen to be the officer in charge. I have met Yuvraj Jaswant too.'

Tara continued, 'Shivani handed me some letters written by Madhubala's suitor. She felt it could help her know more about her sister's suitor.'

Reaching for the box, she removed the bundle of letters. 'As I was reading some of the letters, the dates on them struck me as odd. They go back four years and I was in Baroda back then. I distinctly remember that a girl of marriageable age from a well-to-do family was abducted around the same time. There was a lot of hue and cry and similar instances were reported from the Central Provinces, too. I had a hunch that there might be a connection to other disappearances and, to follow it up, I have been going through newspapers of the timeline when these letters were written.'

Arun was reading the notes and noticed the dates and stories highlighted by Tara.

'Look, the first disappearance is reported in Bhopal in November of 1893. When you read the letters, you will see that Madhubala and her suitor started corresponding around February 1894. However, the disappearances coinciding with the dates of the letter don't begin till about April of 1894. Since then, each letter written to Madhubala is posted from a different town. Looks like the suitor had to travel out of Jaiwar often. The suitor especially signs off saying he would be back soon and was waiting for the day he can ask for her hand in marriage.'

Arun grasped on the theory and read with fascination the crimes around the date on the letters. Each letter corresponded with the abduction of a girl from a different town. The last letter caught his eye.

'This seems to be the Indore case, which I have been studying to get some insight for my current one,' stated Arun.

'An interesting point, Inspector, is, this letter was written two days before the fire at the palace...the fire that took Madhubala's life. She was slated to elope with the suitor that week.'

'Are you saying it is the same suitor who is involved in abducting young girls here in Bombay? But to what purpose?' questioned Arun.

Tara deliberated over his question, while Arun read the letters again to see if they could shed some light. *The dates hold the key to the mystery*, Arun thought.

'I am not sure if it is the same person. It could very well be someone impersonating the original perpetrator. But I do have some good news for you regarding the mystery man the police are seeking. I believe a clerk at Ratanbai School and the mystery man seen with the girls are one and the same. He, I believe, is an accomplice in all this.'

'And how did you come to that conclusion?'

'Well, I remember meeting this young man named Jha at the school, who had dropped the names of the girls when I mentioned I knew them. So you see, Mrs Maneckjee did not exactly break her promise. I was already aware and asked her to confirm their identities.'

Arun pursed his lips in disbelief and nodded her to continue.

'I had never seen this clerk during my time in the school and thought him to be a new member of the staff. Yesterday while I was visiting Princess Shivani, Shankar managed to speak to a few fishermen who had heard a cry for help in the wee hours of the morning, prior to you finding Naina's body. One of them mentioned hearing a different accent, which sounded more from the Central Provinces.'

'I am aware of the accent. The fishermen gave the same information to my constable. They also wondered why they were repeating the information again. It seemed like there was another "constable" talking to them in the morning.' Tara had a look of mock innocence on her face. Arun tried his best not to laugh.

'While we now know that it may be the same person Gauri and Naina knew, how is he connected to Vidya? To add to this confusion, I think Vidya was never meant to be the third girl.'

'What?' A shocked Tara looked into his eyes.

Arun wasn't sure he wanted to divulge the bit involving his cousin, Uma. It was as if he was engaged in a battle with himself. After all, Tara was just an acquaintance and to top it all, she was jutting into his area of expertise. However, she had a keen mind and had uncovered a few crucial clues.

Finally, he spoke. 'I believe it was my cousin Uma who was slated to be abducted. She was unwell and did not attend school that day when Vidya was taken hostage. She had even loaned a set of new clothes to Vidya, which is what she was wearing when she disappeared.'

'That is an unexpected piece of information. I am sorry that your cousin is going through such a tough time. Are you sure she is not aware of this mystery young man?'

Arun nodded. 'She isn't. She would have mentioned it otherwise.'

'Actually it is the mention of an accent that made me think of this young clerk I had met. After all, the kidnapping couldn't have been staged without an insider's help. Maybe Jha was to relay information regarding the girls' everyday movements to his accomplice. Shankar's enquiry confirmed that the clerk hasn't been seen since I visited the school.'

'And you believe the man outside Gauri's house and the clerk are the same? Doesn't it all seem far-fetched?' asked Arun.

A smiling Tara showed a sketch to Arun. 'This is the sketch the police had made of the mystery person, who is also the clerk I met. I had Kajri and some other servants confirm it. *Yes*, it is the same person I met at the school. A person with a Central Provinces accent and a jasmine scent. Is it just a coincidence?'

Jasmine scent again. Arun was astonished. Tara had managed to surprise him all over again. Her theory and the facts he had uncovered so far made sense.

'Kajri confirmed our suspicion this morning. The young chap Naina met on the way to school also had a slightly different accent and used jasmine hair oil.'

'Well that just proves it!' she continued. Beaming with a sense of accomplishment, she started gathering her notes. 'I have asked Shankar to follow up on the clerk. If I get to know anything, I'll send word to you.'

'Why are you involving yourself in this crime? You come from a good family and seem intelligent enough to do what pleases you, then why are you muddling through abductions?'

Here we go again! 'Rao sahib, thanks for admitting my intelligence. I am trying to help, as I would like the concerned families and my teacher to get closure on this. If you don't want my help, you may say so,' said Tara in clipped tones.

Arun let the subject drop and started to gather the papers strewn all over the desk. He noticed reams of papers with happenings of the case and was about to lift it when Tara bundled them up and put them away. Noticing his interest in her papers, she said curtly, 'I don't want to take any more of your time, Inspector. You may leave if you prefer.'

Stuffing the princess's letters back into the wooden box, Tara shut the lid. Arun was instantly drawn to the carving on the lid. 'Is this box yours?'

'No, it is not. It is Princess Madhubala's, I suppose. Shivani handed it to me. Why do you ask?' she asked in a displeased, yet curious tone.

'A part of the carving atop the lid is similar to the incomplete print on the cloth we found clutched in Naina's hand.'

'Are you saying you found a piece of cloth with the royal seal of Jaiwar on it?' Tara was genuinely perplexed. 'Are you now seriously considering that the prince has something to do with all this?'

Tara had known the prince and the royal family for a while. She couldn't fathom the connection the inspector was trying to establish. But in a way, it did make sense. The piece of cloth found could have been part of the royal seal. *But what was Naina doing with a piece of cloth with the royal seal on it?*

'All I am saying at this point is...thank you, Mrs Sethia, for helping me solve a part of the mystery around the cloth.'

Although not pleased with Arun's lack of an explanation, Tara nodded her acquiescence.

Armed with all of Tara's notes that she had made for him and a promise of letting her know of developments in the case, Arun left her to ponder over the new pieces of the puzzle.

thirteen

12 June

The mango seller kept his word. He sent his boy with news to the police station that the prince had returned. Wagh was waiting outside the station when Arun arrived from the Town Hall. Without any delay, they rushed to the prince's office.

Instructing Wagh to speak with the prince's manager and accountant, Arun knocked on the door of the private office. Pausing on the threshold for a second, Arun took in the scene. The prince was writing a letter and he did not look pleased at all. *What has caused Jaswant to be so strung up?* wondered Arun.

'Apologies for bothering you again, Yuvraj Jaswant. We need to have a word,' said Arun. Jaswant looked up from his letter, surprised. Recovering from his moment of discomposure, he motioned Arun inside.

'What brings you here again? I wasn't aware we had a meeting scheduled.'

'Did Puranikjee not mention? I was here this morning. As you were unavailable, I had requested him to send word as soon as you got in. Clearly that is not the case. You have been here for over two hours and we received no word from your manager.'

Jaswant was surprised on hearing Arun's complaint.

'I have more information pertaining to my case that brings me to your doorstep again. I need to view your trade ledgers for the past five years. We believe your ledgers could hold a clue to the case.'

'Are you implying our business or I am involved in some manner in the heinous act of abducting young girls? Have you taken leave of your senses?' The outrage on Jaswant's face seemed genuine.

'Calm down, Yuvraj. I just want to cross-check a few things on the ledgers. If that proves to be a futile exercise, so be it. I can put in a request for a warrant, but that means the search will be more public. I suggest you co-operate unless you do have something to hide,' said Arun in a placating, yet firm voice.

An exasperated Jaswant called for Puranikjee with trade ledgers from 1893 onwards. Dashing to the side cabinet, the prince poured himself a measure of whiskey and settled in his seat. Arun observed the prince. Not much younger than himself, he looked like a man with a lot on his shoulder.

'Whiskey in high summer?' asked Arun. 'Is something on your mind?'

'I wouldn't need this fortification if you hadn't come here slandering the good name of our family,' said Jaswant in an exasperated tone.

'Don't let my questioning intimidate you, Yuvraj. I am not one for slander. I work only on the basis of facts and evidences.'

A not-so-happy Puranik burst into the office with an armload of ledgers. Wagh followed closely behind. Arun and Wagh started combing through the entries in the ledgers, especially pertaining to the dates of the girls' disappearance from the Central Provinces. From the records, they could gather that the trade wagons had always left a day or two before the disappearances. In some cases, no entry was made when the missing cases were registered. Arun was surprised to see there was no trade entry for the day after the fire or for anytime that week.

'Puranikjee, there is no entry for any trade wagons having left Jaiwar in the days after the fire. Did you miss recording the same?'

'It was the week of Diwali and the estate was in mourning. The wagons did not leave for almost ten days. The royal family was bereaved and I doubt business was on Raje's mind.'

Arun looked at Jaswant. He had a shuttered expression. *The grief of losing a sister so tragically must still weigh heavy on his mind.* Arun decided to let the matter rest for a while. There was no evidence to link the royal family to the disappearance here in Bombay at this juncture. Thanking the prince and apologizing for any inconvenience they might have caused his staff, the policemen decided to take their leave.

Puranikjee accompanied them to the door. On returning, he found the door to Jaswant's office ajar. The prince was frantically searching through his cabinets. He definitely had not heard the knock.

'Yuvraj, can I be of any assistance? I could help you with whatever you are searching,' offered Puranik.

Jaswant looked over his shoulders and said curtly, 'Leave me alone, Puranikjee. I don't want to be disturbed.' Taking the ledgers with him, Puranik left, closing the door behind him.

12 June

Mukund returned home that evening to find Tara pacing the corridor frantically. 'What has you so strung up, sister?' he asked.

Tara swirled around and said peevishly, 'I am waiting for Shankar. Hopefully he gets me the information I seek.'

Mukund wondered what had got his usually level-headed sibling so impatient. Settling in an armchair, he picked up the glass of water the servant offered him. Tara came into the room too and looked a bit embarrassed at her earlier snappy behaviour.

'I am sorry, Bhai. How has your day been?' she asked apologetically.

'I am doing fine. Just decided to get home early and stay in.'

'What about Mohan bhai and Baabuji? Will they be home soon?'

'Baabuji has the Cotton Merchants' Association meeting and Mohan has gone to the theatre. He seems to be in love with the new actress on stage,' rued Mukund.

'Maybe I'll write a letter to Vasudha. She must be anxious as her due date approaches.'

'That is wonderful! I am sure Vasudha would love to hear from you.'

Vasudha was the 19-year-old wife of Mukund. Although it was an arranged marriage between two merchant families, Mukund dearly loved his wife and awaited the day he could hold his baby.

'Mukund bhai, you should take some time out and visit Vasudha at her mother's. I suggest we all go there. She will be very happy to see you. If it isn't too modern, you should stay back with her till the baby arrives.'

'I'll think about it. Meanwhile, I am tired of waiting for the baby. I am so worried, she is away. Maybe I can convince her to move to our estate up in the hills. The air there is cleaner than in the city and the Plague hasn't spread to that part yet.'

Radha came in to call them for dinner. She took in the tensed face of her nephew and hugged him. She had always been close to them. Having Radha to talk to was always soothing for all the Desai siblings. She was modern in many ways and the siblings appreciated her presence in their lives. They always wondered how she was able to overcome the societal pressure of a widow managing someone else's household. Since their mother's death, their father was coerced into marrying Radha by many members of the extended family and friends. Both of them however announced that they would not marry each other and let people think what they liked.

Tara always believed her strength to overcome the blows that fate had dealt her with came from Radha.

Shankar came in just as Radha, Mukund and Tara were finishing dinner.

'What have you for me, Shankar?' asked Tara, wiping her wet hands in her sari hurriedly.

'I found the barber of our young clerk. We were lucky. The guy came in just as I was leaving after a quick chat and shave. I waited for him to finish his shave and massage and then followed him to his hideout. Guess what, this young chap lives in one of the hostels of Grant Medical College. On further enquiry, it was revealed he is a student of medicine. His name is Kishen Lal Das.'

'That is such fantastic news, Shankar. You are an absolute gem. What would I do without you?' exclaimed an excited Tara.

'Maybe not poke your nose in other people's affairs,' said Radha, shaking her head disapprovingly.

'Not get involved with crime, for starters. You are such a curious and nosey soul,' said Mukund in a playful tone

'Bhai, if my enquiries can help the police, why shouldn't I?'

'Helping the police seems to be the motivator here,' Mukund bantered. Radha laughed.

'Thank you once again, Shankar. You may rest now.'

Quickly scribbling a note with the details about Kishen, she asked another servant to deliver it to Arun on priority.

There has been a leak somewhere. The exchange is to happen tonight without delay. If he had to be the most powerful and preferred in the trade, he had to show his prowess.

12 June

Arun had just finished his dinner and was mulling over the information that Tara had sent including the mystery man's identity. Just then, there was a knock on the door. His landlord and a young boy of about nine were at the door. 'Rao sahib, this boy claims to have a note for you. As I didn't think he was an errand boy, I decided to bring him here myself.'

Arun thanked his landlord and read the note that was from Omkar. It read:

Rao sahib, I received another note. The informer said he can rescue Vidya and will hand her over to me at midnight. The meeting place is St John Church Cemetery near the lighthouse. I think I am being watched, hence the note with my neighbour's son.

Arun thanked the boy and sent a quick reply along with a coin for his efforts. He wrote:

There is no room for mistakes. We will wait in the shadows. We will not make our presence known till Vidya is safe.

Arun wasted no time and sent out word with the help of his landlord's errand boy. One to the night constables at the station to track and bring Kishen in for questioning and another note to Wagh asking him to meet Arun at his residence at 11.00 p.m. to head to the rendezvous together.

fourteen

12 June

Arun sat down on his bed pondering over all the facts and pieces of information as he waited for the time to pass. He had over two hours to kill.

His latest theory was that the girls who had disappeared since 1893 were never found. What could have happened to them? Could it be they were sold or carted off to some distant land? Maybe that was a possibility? If someone was involved in such a trade, what did he gain by pointing the finger at Jaswant or the royal household? Unless of course someone in the household was involved.

The stress and lack of sleep caught up with Arun and he fell asleep unknowingly. The horrid recurring dream had him gasping for air. The muggy room did not help matters. Opening the window to let some fresh sea breeze in, Arun looked out at the deserted by-lanes of Bombay. The hustle and bustle of the city had died down. Dark clouds crowded the sky and the cool breeze from the sea and docks soothed his sweaty face.

I have indeed come a long way from the life back in Venugiri.

A sudden noise jerked him from his wool-gathering. He quietly turned away from the window and crept towards the door. Someone was on the stairs. The third step before the landing always creaked. The candle had died sometime along his nap. He quietly lit it and proceeded towards the door. Leaving the door unlocked, he stood behind it awaiting the unknown visitor. The doorknob turned and Arun suddenly pulled the door open. The intruder tumbled in with a loud thud. Slamming the door shut, he turned towards the figure, who was now on the floor. 'Show yourself, before I give you a reason to be sorry,' he uttered ominously. The figure turned and in the pale candlelight, he saw who it was.

'You?!' he shrieked.

The cloaked figure hurriedly scrambled to the other end of the room.

'What are you doing here at this hour? It is improper for you to be here or out and about?'

'Please help me. I had to see you. My life is in danger. I had no choice but to come see you.'

Arun walked over to the other end of the room and grabbed a pitcher of water and poured some into a glass. Handing it to the intruder, he said, 'Start from the beginning.'

They heard sounds and clattering of a door opening on its hinges. The girls huddled together. Two men came in. It was too dark to see their faces. 'I am sc...scared,' whispered Gauri. Before Vidya could think of anything, they bound and gagged her. The men then struck Gauri unconscious and placed a hood over her head.

They carried a limping Gauri out and the big door clanked shut, leaving behind a sobbing and bound Vidya.

Arun rushed out of his quarters only to bump into Wagh at the landing. It was almost 11.15 p.m. and Wagh had come looking to Arun's quarters when he did not turn up at the designated spot as promised.

'Wagh, I need you to do something,' said Arun urgently. 'Head to St John Church with our men and stay hidden. Omkar is meeting the abductor there at midnight. Be alert, we need to capture the culprit this time. I will see you there.'

'Don't you worry, Sahib. We will get him this time,' promised Wagh.

'I have an urgent matter to resolve. I am counting on you to apprehend the fellow,' instructed Arun.

As soon as Wagh left, Arun went into his room and said, 'Are you absolutely sure your pursuer did not follow you here?'

'I cannot be certain. All I know is I crossed the road just as the tram turned and, in that split second rushed into this lane. I cannot say if he saw me or not.'

'It will be over soon. But first we need to get you somewhere safe.'

There was a loud rumble and the sky burst open. Arun cursed his luck. The rain was not going to help. Arun bundled his guest in an old raincoat of his and donned one of the new issued ones from the department. They quietly crept down the back stairs and walked into the downpour, keeping to the shadows.

Jaswant had reached home late that evening. It was almost ten. The information he awaited had come in late. The entire household was in a chaos as he entered his residence. 'What is happening here?' he thundered. His housekeeper, one of the old-timers from the palace, stepped forward.

'Yuvraj, Shivani Raje is missing. She stepped out with her maid to go to the sea front. When they didn't return in an hour, I sent out the servants to search for them. The servants found the maid unconscious behind the coconut grove at the end of the beach.'

'There is no sign of the princess. I have already launched a full-scale search party,' his butler Bhim Singh pitched in.

'Why on earth did no one inform me? A phone call to the office is not such a big task.'

'Yuvraj, I had called…' said a bewildered Bhim Singh. 'Puranikjee informed me to start a search immediately and that he would inform you.'

Jaswant was at his wits end. He needed to inform the police. Maybe Inspector Rao would be willing to help. 'Get the carriage out. I am heading to the police station. You continue the search while I get the authorities involved.'

fifteen

12 June

Vidya heard the door open and in the light emanating from the lantern, she saw a figure walking towards her. He quietly swore as he saw her being gagged and bound. Placing his lantern at the far corner of the room, he came closer.

'I am going to let you go,' he whispered. 'You are to make no noise. Is that understood?'

Vidya nodded mutely. Adrenalin was rushing in her blood stream. This was unbelievable. She was going to be set free! He slowly began to remove the gag from her mouth. 'I won't untie you until it is time. It is just a matter of an hour now.' He offered her some water from a pouch he carried. Vidya gladly gulped down the cool water. As the liquid drenched her parched throat, she felt her tense limbs and mind relax.

'Rest well, girl.' It was clear he did not mean well. Vidya was panicking again. She had been drugged. Fear clawed her insides. She may never be able to meet her parents or Omkar again. 'You are going to see some action soon,' he whispered in her ear, and she could feel her heart pound restlessly like it had been all this while, before everything went dark.

12 June

Tara was in her room reading the letters from Madhubala's box. It was quite late in the evening. She had left one of the windows in the far end of the room open to let in the scent of freshly drenched earth. *Oh what a feeling!* Suddenly a line in the letter caught her attention.

Your sketches are always so lifelike. Wish you could send me one of yours as a keepsake the next time you write.

What sketches? Did Madhubala sketch or paint miniatures? Getting out the box, Tara rummaged through the secret compartment in search of any sketch that Madhubala might have hidden. A thorough search yielded nothing. Disappointed, she started placing all the letters and the three pieces of jewellery back in the box when she came across a beautiful pocket watch. It had a carving on the top and an inscription on the inner lid. *Madhubala: September 1894.*

Closing the lid, Tara was about to set the watch back when she felt its lower part to be askew. Turning the piece, she tried to align the bottom to the rest of the timepiece when it popped open. Inside the bottom piece was a beautiful miniature of a striking young man and a woman. The miniatures were both signed '*Mahua*'.

Maybe Madhubala used a different name for her art. 'Oh Madhubala, you were so beautiful!' sighed Tara, looking at the first miniature that had the lady dressed in full regalia including a tiara with the Jaiwar crest. Placing all the jewellery and letters back in the box, Tara continued to stare at both the portraits. There was something familiar about the portrait of the princess that Tara couldn't put her finger on. The young man, on the other hand, was a total stranger. *It could be the suitor,* thought Tara. She put the letters aside and got ready for bed.

It was now pouring outside and the winds clattered the window panes. Tara was in bed, but couldn't sleep. Her mind was still filtering all the information she had on the case. There was a sudden loud knock on the main door.

Quickly draping a dupatta over her skirt and blouse, Tara stepped out of her room. Radha, Mukund, Mohan and Moolchand also stepped out.

'Stay here,' instructed Moolchand while rushing behind his sons to see who it was at the door. Radha and Tara stood at the landing overlooking the main foyer. A servant opened the door hesitatingly and a figure in a black raincoat pushed inside struggling for breath.

'Who are you?' asked Mukund.

The figure dropped the hood and said, 'I am Manjula. I was dropped here by Inspector Arun Rao. My life is in danger.'

Tara gasped. She couldn't believe her eyes. She rushed down the stairs.

'I cannot believe this. It is you. Does your family know?'

Moolchand stepped next to his daughter and said, 'Do you know her, Tara?'

'Baabuji, meet Madhubala, the not-so-dead princess of Jaiwar.'

Omkar arrived at the churchyard as planned. The priest and his students had all retired to their quarters at the far end of the property. There was no one around. The eerie silhouette of a stone church coupled with the rain added to his already strung up nerves. He was nervous about the whole affair and prayed for Vidya's safety.

He looked around, but couldn't make out Arun, Wagh or any of the policemen in the pouring rain. He just hoped they arrived on time to get the culprit.

'Lord, please let Vidya be safe. If I rescue Vidya tonight, we are not waiting for her to finish school. She can study after we marry. I am not letting her out of my sight,' prayed Omkar softly.

The rain intensified and from his vantage point, he could see the newly built barracks across the road. This area had developed massively in the last couple of years, slowly turning into an armed forces stronghold, especially since the military-held fort area had been disbanded. He now had to wait for Vidya to arrive.

∽

It was almost midnight. After dropping Madhubala, Arun boarded the tonga to get to his next destination. Getting off a street before, he instructed the driver to head to the police station and send for backup. He hoped Omkar, Wagh and the others had saved Vidya and nabbed the informer or accomplice, whoever he was. He was crucial in tying up all the loose ends.

Arun recollected all the small clues that he had missed. If only he had paid more attention to all the conversation he had had. He should have reacted to all the small flags that his mind had raised. With all the information Tara and Verma had fed him, he could have cracked this case, without putting Madhubala's or the other two missing girls' life in danger.

On reaching the guest house, he was told the guest was not in. Not knowing where to head next, he stepped out in the rain again when he was ambushed by two men. The last thought on Arun's mind before darkness descended on him was that no one knew he was at Picket Lane.

∽

Vidya started to stir.

Why did I agree to the idea in the first place? I should have borrowed money or found a temporary job or even got married to a rich girl. Why did I let myself be convinced this was a better option.

Sighing, he scanned the area again. Lifting an unconscious Vidya on his shoulder, he trudged along the muddy road towards the bullock cart at the churchyard. So far, Omkar had come alone and he hoped there would be no glitches to his plan.

Although navigating a muddied road with a girl on his shoulder in pouring rain was not his favourite activity, this exchange was essential. He would board the early morning train to Calcutta and leave this city for good in a few hours. Reaching the church, he quickly settled Vidya in the bullock cart and pulled the flaps down to shield her from the rain. Scanning the premises, while keeping to the shadows, he walked towards the awning, where Omkar was waiting. After waiting for five more minutes, just to ensure no one followed him here, he called out to Omkar.

'Are you alone?' he whispered.

A startled Omkar swung around. 'Yes. Where is Vidya? I have got the money. I have not said a word to anyone about the ransom.'

'You are indeed getting better at this. Show me the money.'

'Show me Vidya first. I need to be sure she is well and unharmed.'

'She is in the bullock cart tied to that lamp post,' he said, pointing to the spot where the cart was parked. 'The moment you hand over the money, you both are free to go your way,' he said from the shadows.

He was still to show his face. Omkar had no clue if he could be trusted on his word. There wasn't much he could do anyway. Omkar took out a small pouch from his pocket and threw it towards the man. It however landed a tad bit short. As the man bent down to pick up the pouch, Omkar charged at him and tackled him to the ground. Caught unaware, he bore the first punch that Omkar landed him. Instinctively he pushed Omkar back and rolled away. Omkar came at him again and, this time, he was prepared for the attack. He grabbed Omkar by his collar and tried to strangle him. Omkar tried to wrench away and kicked his attacker in the shins.

'Stop it both of you,' boomed a voice. Three police constables rushed over and separated the men. Thakore had brought lanterns and a pistol. Walking over to the struggling attacker, he shone the light at him.

'Kishen Lal Das, you have a bloodied nose and a black eye. Hope you have learnt enough in Medical College to administer first aid. I would hate to disturb Dr Webb.'

An annoyed Kishen shot Omkar a look of dismay.

'You are under arrest for the abduction of Vidya Naik, Gauri Deshmukh and Naina Rani Mehta and the death of the latter.'

'I did not kill anyone,' cried Kishen. 'I was trying to save the girls. Also, it was not my idea to nab the girls in the first place.'

By then, Wagh came in with a wobbly Vidya in tow. 'I found her in the cart by the lamp post, Sir.'

'Vidya,' yelled Omkar, rushing towards her. 'I was so worried. Are you hurt?'

'I am fine. Just bruised from all the bonding. Thank you so much for saving me,' she said, looking around.

When her eyes fell upon Kishen, her reaction surprised everyone. 'You! Aren't you the clerk Uma used to ask all those medical questions to at school? You told us you were a medical student and working at the school to pay your fees. Why did you abduct me?'

'That,' said Thakore, 'is a tale I am waiting to hear.'

sixteen

12 June

On reaching the police station, Jaswant was informed by the night constable that Arun had left for the day. Narrating his request, Jaswant pressed the constable to arrange for a search for Shivani. The constable patiently explained that most of his colleagues were out on the abduction case and the junior group was awaiting further instructions. Just then, Arun's tonga driver rushed in scattering puddle water everywhere. 'Inspector sahib has asked for backup.'

The night constable and Jaswant looked at the shivering tonga driver. 'Do you know where Inspector Rao is?' asked Jaswant.

The driver was surprised to be questioned.

'I am a friend of the inspector's and need his help,' hedged Jaswant.

On getting a nod from the night constable, the driver replied, 'First, he and a lady got off at a big mansion on Queens Road. Then he returned alone, and I dropped him off near Picket Lane.'

Jaswant asked the driver for directions to the mansion on Queens Road and rushed out, while the night watchman ordered for backup to help Arun.

12 June

Thakore and his men along with Vidya and Omkar gathered around a bound Kishen in the church premises. The constables searched

Kishen for any weapons and combed the area to ensure there were no further surprises.

Kishen grudgingly told his tale. A student of Grant Medical College, he did not secure a scholarship for his last year at medical school. His parents could not afford his fees and his mother had written to her brother to help them out. His uncle had visited him at the start of the summer break and told him he would loan him the amount and maybe more too, if Kishen were to assist him in a small assignment. Kishen had always wanted to be a doctor and agreed to help his uncle. His uncle then paid the fees on his behalf and left town.

'He returned a couple of weeks ago and demanded I help him with some powders that would keep people sedated. I flatly refused to do anything illegal. He convinced me saying he only needed my expertise with medicine to help him. That a friend of his had a hysterical wife and did not want to let it out in society. I agreed to make the drugs, not knowing what I was about to do was wrong. As an aspiring doctor, I should have said no,' Kishen sighed.

'Why did you agree to help him with the abduction?' queried Wagh.

'I did not,' cried Kishen. 'I stumbled upon one such operation by accident. I was working as a part-time clerk at the school when I saw my uncle's servants abduct Gauri. I immediately rushed to her house to let her family know, but got cold feet and ran away from there. On returning to the school, I got to know that Naina had gone missing too and everyone in the school was worried.'

'What was your role, if not abduction?' questioned Thakore.

'I met the girls sometimes on the way to and at school. Unknown to me, my uncle's men kept tab on all our daily activities. My uncle's men abducted both Naina and Gauri and drugged them with the medicine I had prepared. I don't know if ransom was part of the plan. I only know what my uncle told me, when I confronted him.'

Pausing to recollect his thoughts, Kishen continued, 'But things did get messed up the night Naina died. Also, I overheard my uncle yell at his goons saying it was the wrong girl who was picked up at the temple.'

'Oh my God! It was Uma you wanted, not me.' Vidya cried. 'I wondered why I was being held captive; my family is not as rich as Uma's, Gauri's or Naina's.'

'Well, that was an unfortunate mistake, Vidya. Now, Kishen, tell us where is Gauri Deshmukh?' enquired Thakore, turning to Kishen for an answer. 'She is with my uncle. She will be sold to a bidder tonight and my uncle will get his money. The exchange is due at 1.00 a.m. at Bombay Green—'

'Why did you decide to barter Vidya with me?' Omkar butted in. Though displeased with a civilian asking questions, Thakore let it pass.

'I had followed my uncle to the lighthouse, to confront him. At that time, I spotted some men and my uncle coming out with Naina. They were loading her into one of the trade wagons. The next thing I know she has scrambled out from the other side and ran away. All the men, including me, gave pursuit, but I did so discreetly. Unlike my uncle's men, I wanted to help her get away. By the time I caught up with them, it was too late. I saw her fall into the sea. Not waiting for them to spot me, I hid behind a few boulders and then left the hiding place as soon as I spotted some fishermen come along.'

Kishen took a moment to gather his composure before continuing with his tale. 'When I confronted my uncle about the missing girls from the school later, he lied to me that no one was hurt. I was not convinced and threatened to go to the police. He blackmailed me saying it was the drugs that I had prepared that were used to keep the girl sedated. I was already involved and had no choice but to tag along.

'My uncle had ample experience, he said, of doing this before. He, I got to know, was the ring leader of a spate of crimes committed all along central India.'

Wiping the sweat on his forehead, Kishen said, 'That is when I decided to save Vidya from a fate such as Naina's or scores of girls before her. I had seen Omkar with Vidya and Uma. You were my best bet to get away from this mess and hence I wrote that note. The money was for my getaway. It would have helped me to continue my education in some other place away from my uncle's reach.'

'Chavan, take this man to the police station and record his statement,' ordered Thakore.

'Omkar, I trust you will see Vidya home safely. The rest of you, we have a ring to catch and save a girl. Come on, let's hurry.'

seventeen

13 June

Arun could feel the damp earth sticking to the side of his face. It had stopped raining. He slowly opened his eyes. He had a raging headache. The first figure he noticed was that of a bound girl. Surrounding her were a few men. *The girl must be Gauri,* he mused. *Thank God she is safe!*

'Welcome back, Arun. I was waiting for you to regain your senses,' said a known voice from the shadows.

Arun peered in the direction of the voice and said, 'I know the whole story. You can show your face, Shukla.'

Shukla stepped out of the shadows with a lantern in his hand. 'I had so hoped to conclude my affair and board the train tomorrow, without you ever knowing what happened to the girls. And here we are at Bombay Green conducting nasty business in plain sight.'

Arun looked around in the feeble street light coming in through the canopy of trees. He could see the gas lights surrounding the Mint and the Town Hall at a distance. Bombay Green was the original name for this massive park in the centre of the walled city. A beautiful green oasis with paved walkways, large shady trees and cladded drains, the park was the highlight of city planning. Surrounded by ornate buildings, Bombay Green continued to be a favourite haunt of both the locals and the British. A hive of activity in the evenings, it now lay quiet and deserted.

'Naina's death only made matters worse,' Shukla came closer and laughed evilly. 'Your doggedness in ferreting clues and pursuing every angle of the case made it impossible for me to execute my plan. In the midst of all this, one of my associates decided to take matters into his hands. That complicated matters further. If only you could be more like the others, who cared very little for the missing girls.'

Arun was filled with rage. 'How dare you say such a thing? These girls have a family, who pine for them. How can they be forgotten?'

'Rao, you are indeed naïve. Once a daughter is missing and if not found soon, the family prefers her to be dead. After all, she is considered soiled and of no use to the family. She however is of great use to men like me. Many a girl has filled my coffers over the years.'

'I detest you, Shukla. You are nothing but a blotch on humanity.'

Shukla laughed at Rao's anger. Arun's helplessness excited Shukla. He was after all a master strategist and a sharp police officer would not bring him down.

'I am indeed naïve considering I missed so many early clues. You never visited the fishermen and sent me the note just as a diversion. Your accent, which could have been what the fishermen at Colaba Bay heard, the fact that you were conveniently present in Bombay while the crimes took place. I even gave you the benefit of the doubt even after Inspector Verma mentioned the circumstances surrounding your transfer and rise in rank.'

'It is the Raje of Jaiwar who is to be blamed,' sneered Shukla. 'Had he not made a mess of things, none of this would have come to your notice. My partner was hell-bent on taking revenge on the royal family and we decided to use the royal trade wagon to abduct and transport these girls. If ever anyone was caught, the blame would fall squarely on the royal shoulders. We had ensured the trap was tightly set before any exchange.'

'Aren't you the boss? Do you have another evil person directing this entire act?' asked a shocked Arun.

'I am and will always be my own boss,' Shukla laughed aloud. 'A silly slip meant I had to agree to my partner's revenge plan. It started off like that. But don't you worry, it won't be the case anymore. I no longer need him.'

Arun's mind raced to fathom the identity of the mysterious partner. Meanwhile, happy with a willing audience, Shukla continued to regale Arun with their strategy.

'Our strategy was two pronged. Some girls were abducted for a client, while others just for money. In the latter instance, a ransom note was sent to the parents. If they paid up on time, the girls were returned unscathed. If they did not, they were auctioned off to the highest bidder. What happened to the girls after that was never our concern.'

Arun was disgusted with the working of Shukla's brain. He felt revolted at the thought that he shared the same space with a man with no moral compass. He needed answers though. 'How did you get involved with Princess Madhubala? Why her?'

'The idea was to abduct her and demand ransom from the king. It would also mean rumours of her disappearing with her paramour, causing a scandal and a broken engagement. I was to court her in secret. I was to let it slip that I would be in Jaiwar on Diwali and we would elope. We had to ensure the Raje was made aware of the plan. Then we would abduct the princess. Our goal was within reach. She was locked up in the eastern wing, once the rumour of our love affair reached the royal corridors.

'Madhubala, in her eagerness, managed to escape from the palace and came in search of me. This is where the slip happened. It was our bad luck that she stumbled upon our other abductee. She was too clever to not put two and two together. By the time I noticed her, it was too late. My associate knew the police had been informed and would be scouring the area for the missing girl. He instructed us to hide the abducted girl in the basement of the palace's eastern tunnel and then pursue the princess. By the time I caught up with Madhubala, the palace was in flames. I believed the princess to be dead.'

The silence was broken only by the sound of waves and the cricketing of insects.

'So the other girl was buried under the rubble and the body was never found because the tower collapsed during the fire,' whispered Arun.

Shukla continued as if in a trance.

'Imagine my shock when I saw the princess today at the market buying flowers with a young man. I followed her and realized she was indeed the very same. She has changed her appearance and name. I was enraged. Before I could do anything, she spotted me. The look of fear and disgust that I saw was enough for me to decide to do away with her. I bid my time and wanted to throttle her. Lucky girl, she got away from me and reached you.'

'Why would you continue this abhorrent crime, especially after knowing Madhubala was alive and could rat you out?' enquired Arun.

'This plan was already in action. There are many people and a lot of money involved. I was not expecting Madhubala to be alive and in this city. She wouldn't exactly rat me out; after all, her family is the one who would be caught.'

'Money, you see is a great motivator,' taunted Shukla. 'I realized as a policeman, people seldom suspected me to be involved in such an operation. I also had access to many rich, vile men who would pay me handsomely to maintain their precious harems. These girls, who were by-products of the reformist movement, were hardly experienced in the acts of the real world. We employed a few good-looking youths to help us gain their trust, get them abducted when the time was ripe and sell them to the highest bidder. Sometimes, we gave the parents a chance to get them back by paying a ransom.'

'You abducted Vidya in place of a rich girl. What had you in store for her?'

'We always find a bidder for the girls whose parents are unwilling or unable to pay the ransom. I knew that her parents would never pay and she would be forgotten. I have arranged a buyer for her and she'll be sold off tomorrow.'

'You are such a shame to the police force, Shukla.'

eighteen

13 June

A loud banging on the door of the Desai house had Radha remarking, 'Our house is like a train station today.'

The group turned to look at a dishevelled Jaswant enter with his butler in tow.

'Shivani is missing. I fear she has been abducted,' he announced abruptly.

'NO,' shouted Manjula. Jaswant turned around and saw his long-dead sister sitting with a shawl wrapped around her slender shoulders with a cup of tea in her hand.

Shock etched his features and rooted him still. Mukund stepped out to hold onto a shaken Jaswant. Jaswant reached out to Manjula in disbelief. An overwhelmed Manjula could not say much except embrace her brother.

'Yuvraj, please sit. You are drenched,' Tara suggested.

Still shaking his head in disbelief, he took the cup of tea that Tara handed him.

'What happened to Shivani?' asked Tara softly, aware that even though the reunion was much needed, there was something more urgent at hand.

'She went for a walk by the sea front. She was abducted and her maid was assaulted.'

The Desais looked worriedly at each other. The men immediately offered to start searching, when Manjula spoke. 'Bhaiya, it is Shukla. He may have taken her as a bargaining chip so that I don't spill his dirty secrets.'

'Which Shukla are you talking about? The only one I remember is a policeman who came along with Inspector Verma to investigate the fire.'

'Yes, he is with the police,' said Manjula softly. 'Unfortunately, he was also the man I thought I loved.'

Shocked beyond words, Jaswant sat still. *Why did my sister choose a shady policeman to be her partner?*

'Where could he have taken her?' Mohan thought aloud.

'Either he plans on fleeing Bombay or hide her someplace where we might not think of looking for her. At least temporarily till he gets a chance to flee with her,' said Mukund.

'I think he will use the same plan as before. Use the royal transport to get Shivani out of Bombay,' added Manjula.

'There are wagons bound by rail to Mysore. Most of our completed work is stored in the godowns near the docks,' said Jaswant to the room in general.

'Let us split,' suggested Mukund. 'Baabuji and Mohan, you head to the train station. If Shukla plans to flee with Shivani, train is a sure-shot way out.'

'Bhim Singh, you take a few servants and check the godowns,' Tara pitched in. 'I will accompany Mukund bhai and Yuvraj to the docks. We may be able to ask around, the fishermen or dock workers might have spotted something.'

Although Moolchand was not happy about Tara accompanying the men in the night and that too to the docks, she argued that Shivani might need her once they find her. Besides, Manjula was already under a lot of duress owing to her recent scare and in no position to help. Radha was instructed to inform Manjula's husband and family.

Shukla motioned his men to gather around Gauri. Arun had seen them and hence was careful not to make any hasty move. Shukla stepped closer to her and said, 'If you love your life, you will not make a sound and do as I say.' Gauri nodded woodenly. 'There are a couple of men coming to pick you up in ten minutes. You are to go with them and never to contact your family. If you try anything funny, I will not spare you or the inspector.'

Arun frantically worked on his bonds. His head was pounding and his jaw ached from where one of the thugs had boxed him. If he could overpower one of the men, he could use his weapon to round up Shukla and his other henchman.

A carriage pulled up at the other end of the Green and two men stepped down. On reaching the clearing, one of the men quickly stepped forward and handed a pouch. Shukla signalled his thugs to escort Gauri to the carriage.

Just then, there was an utter chaos. Thakore with his retinue of policemen burst through the trees and surrounded the group. Seeing the police, the men in the carriage fled the scene.

'Lower your weapons, gentlemen. You are all under arrest,' bellowed Thakore. 'Shukla, your nephew Kishen Lal Das has ratted you out.'

Shukla immediately seized Gauri and held a pistol to her neck. 'Thakore sahib, if you don't let me go, I will shoot this girl. Her death will be on you.'

Arun somehow managed to stand up, although he was still working on the ropes tied at his wrist. He tried to reason with Shukla, 'Are you crazy, Shukla? You are surrounded. Surrender yourself. Let the girl go.'

'I have worked very hard to build this business. I am not letting anything *go*, just because you ask me to. I have killed before and pulling the trigger is nothing new to me. So do as I say or I shoot,' threatened Shukla.

Arun noticed a figure behind Shukla. A plan formed in his head. He worked furiously to relieve himself from the bonds. Catching Gauri's eyes, Arun motioned her to fall. For once, Gauri understood and did as she was told, without a fuss. She suddenly dropped on her knees.

Without missing a beat, Arun plummeted himself onto Shukla and tackled him to the ground. Pulling the gun from his hands, he pushed Gauri to safety. Throwing the bonds that he was tied with in the direction of the phantom figure hiding behind the bushes, Arun shouted, 'Shankar, you can come out now. Also, please do the honour of tying up Shuklajee.'

Thakore and the constables rounded the crew.

'The game is over, Shukla. You are under arrest for the abduction of Gauri Deshmukh, Vidya Naik and the murder of Naina Mehta,' said Arun, rubbing his chaffed hands.

nineteen

13 June

Tara, Mukund and Jaswant were scouring the docks and the waterfront searching for Shivani and Shukla. After a long futile search, they sat down at the pier. The rain had abated by then. The sea was rough and high waves crashed against the pier walls.

'I should have voiced my suspicions to Inspector Rao,' said a dejected Jaswant. 'He could have helped me. I felt I could handle everything. What will I tell Mother?' He broke down and looked every bit his 24 years. Mukund consoled the young prince while Tara paced putting her thoughts in order.

'Yuvraj, this is no time to lose focus. Tell me everything you remember about the shipments. Have we checked all the shipments or wagons that were to leave today?'

'The boxes for Mysore would be at the station. Hopefully your brother must have checked those. Bhim Singh will check the ones in the godown due to be distributed along the Bombay presidency. Shukla…I always had my doubts about him. I knew he wasn't what he made out to be when I met him during the investigation. Look where he has got us now!'

Tara replayed all the conversations she had had with Shivani and Jaswant with respect to the trade. 'What about the marble inlay dressing table that the oil merchant in Aden had ordered for his third wife?' she suddenly asked.

Jaswant jumped up and twirled Tara in joy. 'Pardon my

behaviour,' he said, gently putting her down. 'That shipment is due at the docks for tomorrow morning. It was brought in this morning for last-minute cleaning. It is still in the office premises. Let us rush there.'

---

13 June

Arun and Thakore were greeted by the night constable and many officers at the police headquarters who had obviously dressed in a hurry. They were informed of Shivani's abduction. Thakore instructed the night-watch team to lock up the prisoners and ushered a handcuffed Shukla and a tired and muddied Arun into his office.

'You better start spilling the beans, Shukla. Earlier this evening, we caught your nephew Kishen Lal and he has given us a very interesting story.'

'Who is your associate? What is the connection with Yuvraj Jaswant?' asked Thakore.

Shukla burst out laughing. 'That young man was so eager to please his father that he never suspected the activities happening right under his nose. I will never work with someone so young and trusting.'

'I know who the culprit is,' said Arun. Thakore agreed to question Shukla while Arun nabbed the associate, and wished him luck. Calling out to Wagh, they both dashed out towards a parked tonga.

---

13 June

Tara and her companions reached the entrance of the prince's office block at the same time when Arun and Wagh jumped out of the carriage.

'What are you all doing here?' asked a confounded Arun.

'Shivani may be in trouble. Someone abducted her this evening,' filled in Tara quickly. 'And we think she is here.'

Looking at Jaswant, Arun said, 'You should have been straight with me. Your sister could have been saved from a horrid experience.'

'Shall we keep the lecturing for later? Let's first save the girl,' Mukund said.

Mukund and Wagh decided to split and look for Shivani in the basement of the building. Arun and Jaswant burst into the latter's office to find Puranik holding Shivani, all gagged and trussed. He turned around with a gun in his hand when the party pushed into the office.

'Let the girl go, Puranikjee, and surrender quietly,' ordered Arun.

'Lock the door, Jaswant, and keep your hands where I can see them,' ordered Puranik.

'Why are you doing this, Puranikjee?' Jaswant asked, locking the door as instructed. 'You have been with us for so long, why this now?'

Puranik gave a nasty look to Jaswant. He pulled a limp Shivani and making her stand between the window and desk, he said, 'What kind of prince are you, if you don't know what prompted me to do this? Your father is the cause for this. Had he not killed my son, none of this would have happened.'

'Your son committed suicide. My father was not responsible for it,' cried Jaswant.

'Your father had him imprisoned for embezzlement. I beseeched your father for forgiveness and even promised to pay him back every rupee that was stolen. He was heartless. I pleaded with him to reconsider. We have been serving the Kaushals for three generations. He however punished my boy. My poor Pratap couldn't handle prison and took his life.'

'I am sorry for your loss, Puranikjee. Don't hold the young

princess responsible for what her father did. Let her go,' urged Arun.

Shivani slowly gained consciousness. She struggled against her bonds. Puranik held her tightly and pressed the gun to her head.

'Puranikjee, please let my sister go. She is innocent,' Jaswant pleaded.

'Aww…the prince is begging,' Puranik said mockingly. 'It is so good to know the royalty is affected too.' Shivani was aghast but could sense grief in Puranik's voice. 'I want to destroy your father just as he destroyed my family. It was my idea to use the trade wagons to transport the girls.'

He tightened his hold on Shivani when she muttered a cry that made Jaswant flinch. Arun held him back.

'No one suspected the royal wagons to carry anything apart from stones and marble artefacts,' Puranik continued.

Shivani could feel fear course through her veins. The man she had known all her life was definitely disturbed. She looked across the room to where her brother and Arun stood at two ends of the desk and besieged them to save her.

'The rumours were all started by me, so was the fire. I saw the look on your father's face when he saw the eastern wing of the palace burn down,' he recounted with a malicious smile.

Jaswant and Shivani were horrified. No one had ever thought in their wildest dreams that this mild-mannered, middle-aged man they had known since their childhood would have such an evil mind. Shivani's eyes filled with tears.

'Shukla has already confessed to the crime and your entire modus operandi is kaput. Don't make me use force,' asserted Arun.

Puranik laughed like a deranged man. 'Shukla was a lowly constable who was on my payroll when I initially started this game for revenge. It was his idea to turn this into a lucrative business. Having a police officer, who was good looking and willing to play a part, was an added advantage. I always knew you were unlike the other police officers, Arun Rao. They only saw what was obvious.

You, on the other hand, were flushing out clues from obscure pieces of information.'

Arun and Jaswant looked at each other and exchanged a knowing look. Arun slowly inched towards Puranik while Jaswant engaged the manager in talk. 'How is it that the ledgers had no information, if you were using it to cart the unfortunate girls?'

'Did you take me for a fool? I maintained a different and clean ledger for your reference. The day the inspector came asking for the trade ledgers, I knew we had very little time to wrap this up. I told Shukla to wind this up and that not everyone in the police force was amoral like him.'

'Why then did Shukla continue with this plan?' Arun inched closer to Puranik and Shivani.

'Shukla however claimed that he had the situation under control. I now realize he was hungry for power and money, and he felt he could hoodwink the police and get away with it. My revenge would have been complete tonight with the princess shipped off and the blame for all other abductions falling squarely on the royal family. Shukla's actions were those of a foolish and overconfident man. It is because of him that I don't get my ultimate revenge.'

'You have had your revenge, Puranikjee. That fire ended Madhubala's life and shattered Raje sahib. Let this girl go,' implored Arun.

'I believe you have indeed moved from your position, Inspector. I may be old, not blind. Now be a gentleman and move aside while I make my departure. One wrong move and I won't hesitate to shoot either of you or the princess here,' he said, brandishing his gun.

Arun noticed a movement and spotted a familiar figure in the window behind Puranik. It took the figure the shortest time to jump down from the window. 'Drop your weapon, Puranikjee', said a female voice. 'My pistol is far superior to yours. Unlike the Inspector, I am not always patient.'

twenty

Two weeks later

It was a sultry afternoon and Arun had just come back to his office. He made himself a cup of tea and sat by the window reading the afternoon edition of the newspaper. There was major cleaning up to do and a lot of loose ends that needed tying up. Wagh, Kareem, Chavan and other constables and inspectors across the Central Provinces worked to gather the evidence on the fifty-odd missing girls and start informing the families.

Arun and Thakore with Inspector Verma communicated with the families of those girls who had either died or had escaped their harems. The search was on to figure their new identities. It was going to be a long road, but most families were keen on knowing about their daughters. The mounting evidence against Shukla and Puranik were enough to build a strong case and Thakore was already in talks with the commissioner and crown prosecutor about the same.

The abduction case had received lot of print space. Some accounts were downright funny. Many claimed they were witness to the abductions and yet never bothered to report them to the police.

A detailed piece in the Perspective section by T.S. Dave caught Arun's eye.

A Dangerous Game of Money and Revenge

The Bombay Police have successfully closed in these past few days the abduction of the three girls' case that had shocked the city of Bombay.

With the killers of Naina Rani Mehta behind bars and the other girls rescued from their captors, law and order has once again been restored.

The girls are united with their loved ones and are looking forward to heading back to school. Mrs Maneckji, the headmistress of Ratanbai School, is glad the ordeal is over and her girls are safe.

Many parents who had pulled their wards out, have now let their daughters go to school. With girls' education still at a nascent stage, an episode like this can have far-reaching effects.

While Inspector Arun Rao refused to comment on the real cause behind the crime, this reporter has it in good authority that there was a personal angle involved. While that remains a mystery for us to solve the abduction episode brings me to my question for you readers.

Is it fair to punish innocent children for crimes committed by their parents?

Send in your thoughts to us.

Arun folded the paper and rubbed his eyes. The question was relevant on many levels. Dave seemed to be goading the people to respond to situations around them. But how did Dave reach the conclusion about the personal angle? The Kaushal family and police had decided to keep the royal connection out of the picture. Arun concluded that Dave must be a good at ferreting information and maybe it was time to meet him soon.

Wagh came in with a note from Tara. He was all smiles. Arun wondered what was written. Curious, he read it aloud.

You are cordially invited to high tea on Saturday at 3.00 p.m. to celebrate the return of Princess Madhubala of Jaiwar, unscathed.

'I assume you have been invited too, Wagh?'

'Not just me, Sahib, Kareem and Chavan too. We are so excited. This will be our first tea with royalty.'

Arun shook his head. Trust Tara to make a celebration of a horrifying experience by mingling classes together.

Epilogue

3 July

The Agashe, Deshmukh and Naik families along with Thakore, the constables and Arun arrived on time for tea at the Desai house. They were awaiting the arrival of some special guests. Radha ushered in Jaswant and Shivani.

'Didi!' exclaimed an excited Shivani. Although the three siblings had met after Shivani's dramatic rescue a few weeks ago, they had not found much time to settle down and talk about the intervening years. Jaswant was busy managing business and giving statements to the police, while his parents made arrangements at Jaiwar before they could visit their children in Bombay. Madhubala and Shivani bonded again and often met at the former's home. Shivani also found a new friend in Uma. The sisters hugged each other and Madhubala turned to Jaswant. She hugged her brother in a rare display of emotion. 'I am sorry, Bhaiya. I had no choice but to flee back then.'

'I understand, Madhubala. While I have been busy these past weeks, I have had a chance to explain to Mother and Father your side of the story. Father and I are also sorry that we weren't there for you when you needed our support and advice.' Now that Shivani was rescued, Jaswant and Madhubala were able to take out some time in between to discuss everything.

'Father is shocked and I am devastated that I couldn't prevent any of this from happening. Losing you has been weighing heavy on all our minds. It is indeed a relief to see you alive.'

Arun, Tara, Mukund and Mohan joined the royal siblings. Arun was curious to know how Princess Madhubala became Manjula. 'How did you escape and where have you been all these years before marrying Krishna?'

'As most of you already know, I had seen Puranikjee and Shukla and their heinous operation in action. I knew my life was in danger.' Pausing, she looked at everyone. Krishna, who was standing behind her, patted her shoulders comfortingly. 'Puranikjee started the fire as soon as I got back to the palace. I realized they were using our wagons to run their operations. On reaching the east wing, I understood that you had not returned from the celebrations,' said Madhubala, looking at Jaswant.

'Unsure how to call for help, I started to write you a letter, but I had no time to explain everything in detail. I told our nanny what had happened and she said she would inform you as soon as you got in. Her son helped me flee the palace before Shukla or Puranikjee could reach me. It was only later that I got to know that the fire was massive, and a few people, our nanny included, lost their lives in it. People died because of my foolishness. I can never forgive myself for that.'

'I heard the commotion and came running to the east wing,' added Shivani. 'That is when your maid pushed me to run back to the western wing. By then, most of the east wing was engulfed in flames.'

'I was shocked to see the east wing in flames upon my early return,' said Jaswant. 'I had had my doubts about your suitor and decided to leave the celebrations early to have a chat with you. I wanted to dissuade you from doing anything drastic. I barely had time to take Shivani to safety before the east wing started to crumble. The guards had to restrain me from reaching you.'

'It was much later that our nanny's son passed me your jewellery box with all the letters. He told me you had left it with him for safekeeping. I was reading your unfinished letter to Bhaiya, but could make no sense of it,' said a sombre Shivani, recollecting the horrid time in her life.

The group fell silent. With each sibling trying to fathom the enormity of what had occurred and how life was actually so fragile.

'If it is any consolation, Princess, your brother just wanted you to be happy,' said Arun, breaking the ice. 'He thought he failed you and has been carrying the guilt and secret since then. You fled. They recovered the body of a young woman in the rubble. Assuming it to be you, she was cremated. We now know it was the girl who was abducted that night, the one you saw with Shukla.'

Madhubala thanked Arun and asked Krishna to join her at the settee. She continued with her story and told them how she had managed to escape from Jaiwar and reach Baroda to stay with her maternal aunt. Their maternal aunt was married to the treasurer in the princely state of Baroda and seemed like the only refuge at that time. That was when she met Krishna and eventually married him.

'How is it that no one suspected your true identity during your stay in Baroda?' asked Tara.

'Krishnajee and I first met at Baroda, when the Agashe family visited our uncle during Navaratri last year. By then, Maasi had come up with a plausible story. Apart from them, no one else knew my true identity. Maasi never visited our parents with the children in tow. She always made up excuses for not taking us along to meet them. She never invited our family to Baroda for the three years I lived with them. I was to be the governess to our young cousins and help with the running of the household in her absence. I even learnt the local language and tried to do away with my accent.'

'That is where I remember meeting you,' said Tara, realizing why the portrait seemed familiar to her. 'It was at the dinner your uncle and aunt hosted for Diwali. While you didn't speak much, I saw the way you handled the children and was really impressed.'

'She tried to stay away from the limelight. I, on the other

hand, was smitten with her and wanted to get to know her better,' added Krishna, taking on the tale from his wife. 'I always found some reason or the other to visit her. Initially she was hesitant, but eventually she gave in and agreed to marry me. In fact, she speaks the local tongue flawlessly. It is what surprised me, especially when she confessed being the princess of Jaiwar.'

'Krishnajee knew I was the princess of Jaiwar. I never concealed anything from him. We just decided not to drag the family into my murky past. I had already changed my name to Manjula when I lived in Baroda and we decided to continue with it.'

By now, most of the other families and guests had gathered around the royal siblings and were earnestly listening to the fascinating story of Madhubala's escape and subsequent help in solving of the abduction in Bombay. Shrikanth and Mina were beaming with unconcealed pleasure especially now that everyone knew their connection to a royal family. Uma still couldn't make out what the fuss was all about.

Krishna continued with the tale, 'When Baba was transferred to Bombay, I quit my job in Baroda and we moved here to stay closer to the family. Also Manjula and I felt she would be safer in a big city, where the chances of anyone knowing her past would be less.'

'I am so glad you are alive and have found happiness. There is nothing more that I want for you,' said an emotional Jaswant.

'Mother and Father will be so happy to meet you after all these years, Didi. Do say you will visit them, now that everything is out and your life is not in danger.'

The servants came in with tea and snacks and the guests got busy helping themselves to the delicious spread.

Arun stood holding his cup of tea, 'I really need to thank all of you who have helped me and the police in solving this crime and putting the criminals behind bars. My biggest appreciation is to a certain someone for turning up on time to save our lives, that too with a theatrical prop.'

Tara looked up at Arun, who was just about to take a sip of his tea. 'Why do you assume it was a prop? It was my own pistol. I am a keen markswoman, thanks to my hunting sessions in Baroda.'

Arun choked on his tea. The entire group had mixed reactions from gasps to laughter. Recovering from the shock and embarrassment at this new revelation, Arun wiped his mouth and looked at Manjula for a diversion.

'Most of all it is to you, Princess Madhubala, for having the courage to confront your past and tell me the story. Hope you have nothing else to reveal.'

'It is Manjula Agashe, Anna. That is who I am today. I am not giving up my identity again.'

Gradually, the Kaushals and Agashes split to mingle with the other guests. Moolchand and his sons were busy talking to Thakore. The mothers comforted each other as they shed tears of happiness of getting their daughters back. Gauri, Uma, Vidya and Omkar were seen talking animatedly.

Arun sought out Tara, 'May I have a word with you, Mrs Sethia?'

Tara nodded and ushered him to the veranda. A cool sea breeze was blowing.

'Could I request you to please refrain from divulging such information in public so dramatically?'

Tara looked up at Arun with a twinkle in her eyes, 'Of course, Inspector Rao. I was just setting the record straight that I know how to handle a gun.'

'How can I thank you, Mrs Sethia?' sighing Arun continued. 'Your inquisitiveness and knack for getting the right information were very useful in cracking this case. Your daredevil act during Shivani's rescue though unwise, was enough for the prince and me to overpower Puranik.'

'While I understand your bowing to my father's command of not dragging my name in the public sphere pertaining to the case, never imagine even for a moment that I won't repeat what I did that day. I will never hesitate to use a weapon, especially if a life is in danger.'

'Thank you for saving our lives, Tara bai,' said Arun sincerely. 'I sincerely appreciate your contribution in this case, including this grand gesture of arranging high tea with the royalty.'

Tara smiled. This earnest and always-in-control inspector finally called her by her given name. 'I for one am glad the girls got back home safe. They are fortunately recovering fast from the trauma of the last few days. As for the tea, it is just a gesture of appreciation to everyone who played a role in the capture of Shukla and Puranik.'

'That is so true. I still can't believe that you joined the dots between the crimes and letters written to Madhubala. However, it was Shankar who identified Kishen for us. You seem to have a knack for sniffing out criminals.'

They lapsed into a comfortable silence. The hum of voices from the living room filtered through the open doors.

'I also appreciate your family for letting Manjula into your home, especially when all she had were my instructions. I know it was very presumptuous of me to offload her at your doorstep without an explanation.' Tara accepted his thanks.

'You really are on a roll when it comes to thanking us all,' she teased.

Arun, smiled, a little embarrassed. After all, this case had been a lot different from the previous ones he had solved. This time, when it really mattered, civilians had all pitched in to solve a crime and that was an eye-opener for him. 'Yes, it was presumptuous of you. Although it was Radha maasi who was upset with so many people knocking on our door at odd hours. She even commented about our home resembling a station platform.' Arun chuckled at Tara's rendition of Radha's observation.

'She is a very brave woman…Manjula. I am proud she is a part of our family now. Although I am not sure how my aunt is going to deal with this new information now. I am positive she will never be able to stop bragging about the royal connections,' said Arun ruefully.

'I am confident Manjula will handle your aunt. She has truly transformed into an accountant's wife.'

'Thank you for listening to my theories and letting me contribute to solving this case. If you would like my assistance in any of your future cases, Rao sahib, I would be more than willing to help out.'

'Do you plan to stay here for long?' Arun asked shyly. 'Won't you be returning to Baroda soon? How then can you assist the police here?'

Tara understood where his questions were coming from. She had never divulged the real reasons for her helping out in this case or why she was at her father's place. Finally after two years of soul-searching she was getting somewhere and was not ready to give up on her new-found quest. She decided to come clean with Arun.

'Baroda is in my past. Bombay is my home now. I am a widow.'

Acknowledgements

You possess a rare skill which only a few have—creativity. Make the best use of it. These words by Vishal, my husband, is what propelled me to take up on my dream and begin my journey as an author. The journey has definitely not been easy, but I wouldn't trade one minute of it for anything. I would not be where I am today but for the support that I have received along the way.

Sincere thanks to Adit Chouhan, for introducing me to the publishing world and paving the way for my story to reach the world. To the team at Rupa Publications (India) for giving me this chance to realize my dream. Thanks to my editors and the cover designer, for all their inputs and efforts in putting this book together.

This journey wouldn't have begun without my critiquing partner, Krishnan, my father-in-law, who did not mince words and helped me through the numerous drafts and stages of this book. Thanks, RK pa. Tarika Vijayaraghavan and Maulik Trivedi, for being my sounding board, feedback team and always encouraging me to aim higher.

And to my wonderful family for encouraging me to believe in myself and look ahead. A big shout-out to all my friends around the world who have joined me on this journey and given their generous support along the way.